TRAIL TO LOVE

GREAT WAGON ROAD
BOOK THREE

SUSAN F. CRAFT

WILD HEARt
BOOKS

ISBN-13: 978-1-963212-01-3

PRAISE FOR SUSAN F. CRAFT

In *Trail to Love*, Book 3 in her Great Wagon Road Series, Susan Craft affectingly portrays the hardships and perils travelers on the Great Wagon Road endured. Anne Forbes and Michael Harrigan are drawn together as they search for a lost child, care for fellow travelers suffering from smallpox, navigate difficult relationships, and deal with the rough wilderness terrain. When Anne accepts Michael's invitation to settle in his North Carolina town, conflicting ambitions force them to question whether their love is stronger than their differences. Beautifully written and historically accurate, *Trail to Love* features engaging and realistically portrayed characters, vividly drawn settings, and an uplifting faith theme.

— J. M. HOCHSTETLER, AUTHOR OF *THE AMERICAN PATRIOT SERIES*

In *Trail to Love*, Susan Craft weaves a charming story of romance, faith, and adventure as Michael Harrigan, a lumberman, and Anne Forbes, a tailor, are part of a caravan that travels the many miles down the Great Wagon Road in the mid-eighteenth century. This riveting tale of challenges and choices, grief and gratitude, danger and determination is a page-turner with a satisfying ending.

— JANET GRUNST, AUTHOR OF *A HEART SET FREE, A HEART FOR FREEDOM*, AND *SETTING TWO HEARTS FREE*

I dedicate Trail to Love to my children, Allison and Donovan. God blessed me with these amazing, intelligent, and kind people, who share my quirky sense of humor. They enjoy playing Jeopardy and Trivia with me, calling ourselves the queens and king of useless information.

Most importantly, they love Jesus, which means we will continue loving each other throughout eternity.

INTRODUCTION

The Great Wagon Road spanned from Philadelphia, Pennsylvania, through Virginia, North Carolina, and South Carolina and ended in Augusta, Georgia. It began as a path carved out of the wilderness by thousands of bison and deer moving from one water source and salt lick to the next. Indians used the footpath for hunting and for warring against neighboring tribes. Hernando de Soto is reported to have trekked part of the trail during his exploration of the Southeast in the 1500s. Europeans, many of them landed gentry, made new fortunes trapping deer and selling the hides along the road. In the 1700s, the road expanded into a major thoroughfare traveled by immigrants, a large number of them Scots-Irish. Colonel George Washington and his troops traversed the road during the French and Indian War. Over time, the Great Wagon Road had many names. Among them were Great Warriors' Trail, Indian Road, and Valley Pike.

Come, journey with Anne Forbes, a tailor, and Michael Harrigan, a lumberman, as they bestow upon the Great Wagon Road a new name, *Trail to Love*.

CHAPTER 1

1753

*M*ichael Harrigan stepped out of the Pig's Tail tavern and reeled as a blast of torrid air hit him squarely in his face. The heat had not abated even as dusk approached. Someone watching might think him drunk, though he had enjoyed a generous portion of beef pie, cheese, and bread chased with only one tankard of ale. Customarily, he ate a small supper, but he would leave Philadelphia in a few days on a wagon train, and meals akin to the one he had just consumed would not exist on the trail.

He walked off the tavern porch onto the dirt road and headed to the inn where he and his sister-in-law, Megan, and her friend, Amelia, lodged. He had never cared for Megan, especially the way she treated his brother. Cal deserved better. From the moment Michael met Amelia as she disembarked from the ship that had transported the girlhood friends from Scotland, he found her beautiful yet frivolous.

But then, no woman could ever compare to his Heather

with her lovely smile, sparkling eyes, and warm, generous nature. He circled his fingertips over his aching heart. Strange how grief slammed into him sometimes as strong as when she had passed. The smallest things triggered his sadness—the smell of roses, an emerald-green dress the same hue as her eyes, the strumming of a mandolin—an instrument she had often played sitting on their front porch—and singing haunting mountain songs.

He shook his head, freeing himself from the painful reverie. Many responsibilities lay ahead, mainly the two women he had been enlisted to escort back to his and Cal's Blue Ridge Mountain home. Amelia and Megan valued their creature comforts, which did not bode well for their three-hundred-mile trek.

Trouble ahead.

The two women had refused to accompany him to what they considered a questionable part of the city and insisted on a meal served to them in their room. The Pig's Tail was near the docks in an area that required caution, but the fare was excellent enough to overcome any concern.

A child's whining echoed through the street. Two blocks down, a young lad yanked on the petticoats of a woman paused on the corner. She jostled a sleeping toddler with one arm and tried to manage the boy with the other. Frowning, she searched one way and then the other.

Farther down the street, a handful of sailors and a couple of ruffians headed her way.

Michael hurried to her side, but she flinched, eyes wide with fear.

He pulled off his tricorn and held it to his chest. "I mean you no harm. This is not a safe place. You are lost?"

Average looking rather than pretty, she reminded him of a wren—brown eyes, brown eyebrows, brown dress. Her mobcap completely covered her hair that was probably the same unremarkable hue as her brows.

Still wary, she took a moment to respond. "This city is like a rabbit warren. I made a wrong turn somewhere, and I can't seem to find my way back." Her pleasing, velvety soft voice held an English accent flavored with a hint of Scottish brogue.

The two groups of men passed around them without commenting, though one of the sailors ogled the woman.

The little boy wrapped his arms around her knees and whimpered.

She rumpled his hair. "David, dear," she coaxed, "please be patient. We'll be home soon."

Her smile brightened her face and lit her eyes. Between it and her comely figure, Michael rethought his first impression of her as plain. Despite their difficulty, the three of them presented a sweet picture. Her husband was a fortunate man.

Michael swept his tricorn to the side and made a slight bow. "I would be happy to escort you. Where are you going?"

Her candid eyes sized him up from head to toe, locking with his own gaze for a moment. He withstood her scrutiny and attempted to maintain an open expression.

Did his frockcoat bear remnants of his meal? Had his cravat remained neatly tied?

Her shoulders relaxed. He had passed muster.

She gave him a tremulous smile. "Applegate Street. We are staying at an inn there."

Her trust warmed him. "I know it. We're staying on that street as well."

The toddler curled on the woman's shoulder wriggled awake and started crying, increasing the frustration on her face.

Michael knelt eye to eye with the young lad attached to her petticoats. "David, is it? How would you like to hop on my shoulders?"

When the boy's eyes lit with delight and he reached up his arms, Michael glanced at the woman. She hesitated a moment and then nodded. He donned his hat and swung David onto his shoulders. The boy dangled his legs on either side of Michael's neck and banged on his tricorn with his fists.

Michael motioned down the street. "This way."

As they wended their way through dirt streets, some no wider than an alleyway, she avoided eye contact and kept a wary distance, constantly glancing at the little boy now clasping his hands around the sides of Michael's beard. The toddler in her arms continued to caterwaul, precluding any communication.

"My dear laddie, do not fash so. Please, will you not calm down? You will make yourself ill." She hiked the child onto her hip and rubbed his back.

How did a body as small as his make such a racket?

Michael maintained their forced silence until they stepped out onto a wide brick-covered thoroughfare.

Someone yelled, "Cleaning!"

Michael gently pushed the woman up against a store wall and positioned himself in front of her moments before gallons of water gushed out of a pump a few yards away. The water shot across the bricks, carrying dirt and debris down the side gullies.

The woman gasped. "What?"

He stepped away from her and the faint aroma of lavender that wafted about her. "They clean the brick streets twice a day. Nice custom, don't you agree?"

"Nice, but surprising."

There it was again, the lovely soft tone of her voice.

They walked another block before she stopped in front of a two-story clapboard building surrounded by a white picket fence.

The toddler quieted, but not before beads of sweat formed across the woman's brow. She retrieved a handkerchief that was tucked in her under-pocket and dabbed her face. "We're staying here. I can't thank you enough...Mister?"

Michael lowered David to the ground and bowed. "Harrigan. Michael Harrigan."

She jostled the toddler and managed an awkward curtsey. "I'm—"

"Anne! Where have you been?" The question came from a young woman who threw open the gate and stood with her hands jammed onto her hips. Her golden ringlets that curled out from her mobcap bobbed from her irritation. Her blue eyes and creamy skin reminded Michael of the doll he had purchased for his daughter many years ago. "You've had us worried sick!"

"That was *not* my intention, Gail." Flint replaced the velvet in her tone. The ordinary woman with the soft voice had backbone.

"Well, hurry in. We've already begun eating, and we must leave in an hour." She grabbed David's hand, and her mouth twisted into a frown as she finally acknowledged Michael's presence. "You've brought a stranger with you?"

"This is Mr. Harrigan. I became lost, and he was kind enough to help me find my way back."

The blonde made a token curtsy. "You have our gratitude, sir, but we must make haste. Come, Anne. Let's not dawdle."

Anne glanced at him with an apology as she allowed herself to be bustled through the open gate and down the walkway. The color of her expressive eyes—coffee shades with amber flecks—reminded Michael of the white oak acorns so favored by mountain deer.

No, she was definitely not an ordinary woman. Would they cross paths again? What difference would it make? She was a wife and mother.

He strolled toward his lodgings, preparing his mind for the important meeting ahead.

～

*T*hroughout their hastily consumed meal and during the entire time Anne changed clothes, her sister-in-law harangued her for getting lost, for putting her sons in danger, and for being late.

Anne tried to explain that she had intended to take the boys out only for a short stroll. They had become unbearably cranky and irritated with their new surroundings and needed fresh air. They had enjoyed playing in a nearby little park until Anne spotted rows of shops that drew her as a bee to nectar. One store sold only bolts of material that filled shelves lined to the ceiling. Another featured buttons, beads, feathers, and embellishments. Anne had never seen so many hanks of thread in one place. She had not taken the boys inside the shops, but had stood before each peering through the windows, her fingers itching to start a new sewing project. It was not long before she became lost.

Overwrought, Gail did not heed Anne's explanation. She was not normally a harridan, though she liked her own way. Anne was hard pressed not to mention that she loved her nephews as if they were her own children and would give her life to keep them safe. During the lecture, Anne's brother, William, wisely found somewhere else to be.

An hour later, after a maid arrived to care for David and Keith, Anne left the inn and, carrying a lantern for their return, took her place behind William and Gail.

Her brother and sister-in-law made an attractive couple. William's sable-brown hair, brown eyes, and dark complexion served as a foil to Gail's porcelain-doll blonde features. Of medium height, they looked trim in their latest fashions— Gail's solid blue overskirt and penrose-patterned bodice, and William's tan breeches and brown waistcoat—all tailored by Anne. Their handsome appearance made her proud of her work.

Ahead of them, Mr. Harrigan exited an inn escorting two women, one on each arm.

Her heart skipped at the sight of him. Why?

The finely dressed women were engaged in a lively conversation. Which one was his wife?

Mr. Harrigan was certainly an attractive man, and his choice of attire was impeccable. To Anne's tailor's eye, his dove-gray frockcoat perfectly fit his broad shoulders and trim waist. Someone very skilled had fashioned his clothing.

Gail frowned at Anne over her shoulder. "Are you certain about where we are going? Especially in light of what happened today?"

Anne fought the urge to roll her eyes. "I am. I checked the map the wagon master left for us at the inn. We follow this street until it ends at the city boundary and a large field where the wagons will assemble."

As Anne, William, and Gail neared the city limits, Mr. Harrigan and his companions headed in the same direction. Would he be traveling with the wagon train? Anne's arms tingled.

He answered that question when he guided the women off the road and across a two-acre field to join a group of people gathered inside a circle of wagons and tents.

The moment he spotted Anne standing near him, he regarded William, raised an eyebrow, and then greeted her with a nod and friendly smile. The smile lit his hazel eyes and crinkled the fine lines at his temples.

Why did he appeal to her? Wasn't he married to one of the women with him? What difference did it make if he joined the wagon train?

She had made a life for herself caring for her brother's family. She had not thought of love or marriage since her fiancé had passed nine years ago. His death had broken her heart, though the pain had abated over time, and, disturbingly, his visage was becoming a distant memory.

Marriage...children. Was that desire still alive, after all?

CHAPTER 2

*S*tanding with the people assembled inside the circled wagons, Anne regarded the two men facing them.

The taller of the two, in his fifties, tapped his fingers against the side of his tricorn. "Good evening, ladies and gentlemen. I am your wagon master, Aaron Cooper, and this"—he pointed to the younger man at his side—"is Paul Sanders, our scout."

Mr. Cooper wore a brown frockcoat, light-brown waistcoat, and beige breeches. His sandy-brown hair was secured with a ribbon and draped over the back of his neatly tied cravat. His clothes were not as well made as Mr. Harrigan's. Judging by his apparel, if Anne had passed him on the street in the city, she would never have guessed him to be a rugged wagon master. He carried himself with the confidence and ease of a man used to giving orders. She caught the expression in his dark-gray eyes for a second and liked the kindness in them.

Mr. Sanders, a muscular man in his twenties, wore canvas breeches, knee-high boots, and a trade shirt with suspenders. A hawk feather was tucked into the band of his black slouch hat. His boots, though clean and brushed, had seen much wear.

They both inspired Anne's confidence. Her family would fare well in their care.

Mr. Cooper bowed. "On behalf of the Norton Traverse Company, I welcome you. According to your contract with them, Mr. Sanders and I will spend the next three days teaching you a list of skills—driving a wagon, making camp-fires and cooking, and firing weapons. For those not already proficient. We'll also inform you of some of the hazards you might encounter on the trail. I would caution you to limit your cargo. We'll be traversing foothills and mountains that tend to get a lot of rain, which means mud and swollen rivers. It will be to your advantage to carry as light a load as possible. If not, on the trail, I may order you to discard some of the weight."

Anne balked at that news, and she chewed on her bottom lip. She had planned for every square inch inside the wagon. What would they leave behind? William's precious barrel of ink and her trunk of tailor's tools and materials were more precious than gold. Would they discard Gail's bureau that belonged to her grandmother? Or David's rocking horse?

Worrying over it today was not doing any good. They would make those decisions when necessary.

"For now, please, let's get acquainted." Mr. Cooper pointed to one side of the group. "If you would each introduce your-selves and tell us your destination."

A lanky young man nodded and put his arm around the waist of the petite, red-haired woman at his side. "I'm Ezra Banks and this is my wife, Claire. We are flax farmers. That is, I farm, and my wife makes lace from the flax." He smiled down at her. "She makes the finest lace I've ever seen." His wife's face flushed, and she ducked her head. "We'll be joining our family in the northeast part of the South Carolina colony."

One by one, the remaining families introduced themselves. Mr. and Mrs. Smythe and their two young girls headed for Georgia. Two families, the Waters and the Hudsons, farmers on their way to claim free land grants in the South Carolina back-country. Mr. Johnson, a cordwainer hoping to set up a shop at the end of the trail in Augusta, Georgia. The Daniels brothers and their wives who planned to establish farms in the north-west corner of South Carolina. Mr. and Mrs. Tanner, goat farmers who had purchased land in Georgia. Their herd of six goats would travel with the train.

Anne made a mental note to approach the Tanners about bartering her tailoring services in exchange for milk for her nephews along the way.

When Mr. Harrigan stepped forward, Anne perked up.

"I'm Michael Harrigan, and this is my sister-in-law, Megan Harrigan, and her friend, Amelia Stanford. My brother and I own a sawmill and logging company in Graniteville in the North Carolina Blue Ridge Mountains. We're headed home."

He was not married to either woman, though the golden-haired one had sidled close and slid a possessive hand around his forearm. Interesting.

Anne's brother greeted the group next. "I'm William Forbes. This is my wife, Gail. We have two small boys, David and Keith. I am a printer intending to join a printing company in Camden, South Carolina." He motioned to Anne. "And this is my sister, Anne Forbes."

Anne curtsied and smiled to the group.

Mr. Harrigan pivoted Anne's way, studied her, and then tapped the brim of his hat. His scrutiny prodded her to check her mobcap for stray curls.

What was it about the man that made her so aware of him... of herself?

Mr. Cooper folded his arms across his chest. "Thank you for your introductions. There'll be plenty of time on the trail to make each other's acquaintance, but let's address the matters at hand." He motioned toward the wagons. "I've assigned each of our ten families a number. There's an invoice attached to each wagon with your name and the list of supplies that will be delivered to you tomorrow. The invoice also has your designated number on it. Each day, based on that number, we will rotate the order of wagons. That way, you'll share being on the tail end of the train eating everyone's dust."

Several people chuckled.

Mr. Cooper pointed toward the edge of the clearing. "As you can see, we have horses enough for each wagon. We'll start getting to know how to handle them at dawn tomorrow. Meantime, please, take this opportunity to get familiar with your wagon."

Anne found theirs at the opening of the circled wagons and perused the invoice nailed to the bed. William and Gail stood behind her.

"We are number ten." Anne ripped the paper from the nail and scrolled her finger down the list. "Two bags of flour. Twenty pounds of bacon. Two pounds each of tea and coffee. Ten pounds each of sugar and lard. In addition, there are sacks of rice and beans, plus dried apples and peaches. The list is correct, William."

He stared at the paper and frowned. "It seems a remarkable amount of foodstuff."

"It does." Anne folded the paper and slid it into her underpocket. "But, as the letter we received from the Norton Company indicated, we will run out long before the end of the trail, and we should plan to purchase more supplies from settlements and farms along the way."

Gail clasped William's arm. "We have enough funds?"

He patted her hand. "Don't fret, Gail. Anne and I planned this journey down to the smallest detail. Including enough Spanish dollars to see us through." He moved closer to the wagon wheel. "Now, shall we explore inside? Though I'm not sure how we enter."

"May I be of assistance?" a voice called out from behind Anne.

Mr. Harrigan waited a step away from her. His companions conversed with several other ladies beside their own wagon.

Anne sidled toward her brother. "This is Mr. Harrigan, the gentleman who helped me find my way back to the inn."

The men bowed to each other

"I am grateful for your assistance. I know we made introductions to the group, but I am William Forbes." William put an arm around Gail. "This is my wife."

Gail furrowed her brows and curtsied. "Yes, we met briefly."

William gave his most charming smile. "In light of our closeness on the wagon train, may we be less formal with our names?"

Leave it to her endearing, cordial brother to encourage friendships.

Mr. Harrigan pressed a hand to his chest. "I would be happy to. I'm Michael."

Anne had always favored the name Michael.

"My wife is Gail, and my sister is Anne." Her brother motioned to each of them.

"I look forward to getting better acquainted." Michael moved to the back of the wagon. "If I may, I'll show you how to get into the wagon."

He loosened the latches on either side of the backboard, which allowed the piece of wood to fold open. "Once you've opened the backboard, you use the spring step"—he pointed to a foot-sized block of wood to the right of the back wheel— "here. It's best to put your left foot on it. Grab this brace. Then step up onto the backboard." Following his own instructions, he sprang up onto the panel.

William joined him and held out his hand to Gail.

Gail giggled. "I'm not certain about this."

In a moment, he swept her up and into the wagon.

Michael offered his hand to Anne, who lifted her skirts, placed her foot on the step, and was hauled so close to his body, his warm breath feathered against her face. The calluses on his palm rubbed against her fingertips. Working man's hands, heavily tanned and scarred, though gentle.

Gail pinched her nose. "What is that smell?"

Anne breathed in and wriggled her nose. "It reminds me of cod liver oil."

Michael stooped over to walk farther inside. "It's linseed oil. They soak the bonnet...the canvas...with it to make it waterproof. The slats in the wagon bed have been caulked with tar to make them waterproof as well. The odor should abate in a few days, once the cargo is loaded."

Gail fanned her face. "It can't abate soon enough for me. Come, William, let's go back outside."

When they departed, Michael motioned toward the back of the wagon. "May I assist you?"

Anne shook her head. "I'm staying for a few minutes. I plan to sew pockets to the sides of the canopy...the bonnet...for extra storage. I need to take measurements." She pulled a pencil and strips of measuring paper from her apron pocket.

"How do you propose to do that?"

She touched one of the wooden hoops supporting the canvas. "I'll sew two pieces of linen together along three sides, leaving one end open. I'll stretch the pocket from one rib to another and secure them with string ties." She looked up at the canvas ceiling. "The pockets will have to be fashioned toward the top, since the cargo will be stacked high."

"What a fine idea. Ingenious." He splayed his hand across the canvas. "Megan and Amelia refuse to pare down their luggage. I've never seen so many hat boxes. Would you be willing to make some pockets for my wagon? I could use the room. I'd be happy to pay you."

Anne could not resist the eagerness in his hazel eyes. "I'd be willing to do that."

"Thank you, Anne."

He looked so pleased, Anne had to resist reaching out and cupping the side of his soot-black beard.

"You'll let me know how much I owe you?"

She spread the measuring paper across one side of the canopy. "I will."

"I'll leave you to it." He walked to the end of the backboard and jumped down.

Only a few minutes passed before she heard voices outside.

"How should I manage this, Megan? Michael doesn't seem remotely interested in me," said a woman Anne was certain must be Amelia.

"Patience. All men enjoy being made to feel special. Michael will require extra attention. He has never fully recovered from his wife's death. He has a nine-year-old daughter, Cate, whom he adores. So once we reach Graniteville, you can form an attachment with her. Win his heart that way."

Their voices faded as they passed by the wagon.

Amelia had set her cap for Michael. It was not any of Anne's business. Why did it disturb her so much?

CHAPTER 3

*T*ry as she might, the following morning as Anne learned how to harness the draft horses and to drive their wagon, she could not stop watching the interactions between Michael and Amelia.

The woman flirted shamelessly, gazing up at him and fluttering her eyelashes. To Anne's surprise, Amelia had agreed to learn how to drive their wagon. She managed to appear dainty doing even that—tucking herself as close as she could next to Michael on the wagon seat and asking his help to wrap the reins around her hands that were encased in the most ridiculous lace gloves, so unlike Anne's practical black leather ones. Throughout the morning, Amelia took every opportunity to jump down from the wagon and into Michael's arms. She practiced her charms on him as a spider spinning its web around its helpless prey. Only, this victim enjoyed her beguiling ways, laughing loudly and often at her sweet talk.

At midmorning, the delivery of their provisions as well as their belongings from the ship took Anne's mind off Michael. With William on the other side of the clearing firing a musket, and Gail chatting with a group of women learning how to cook on a campfire, the loading of the wagon fell to Anne. It was just as well, since she had drawn the diagrams for the placement of their cargo.

The porters who brought their belongings from the ship made quick work following her instructions and packing the wagon with the furniture, larger storage trunks, and William's printing supplies toward the front, boxes with bedding and everyday changes of clothes toward the middle, and food and cooking items and medicine kit at the rear of the bed. They left a narrow corridor down the middle for easy access to the cargo. Tired, but satisfied with the progress, she bade them goodbye and sat on the backboard, dangling her legs over the edge.

At the western end of the field, a group of wagoners gathered around Michael. Curious, she left the wagon and stood at the back of the crowd.

Michael removed a short branch from the top of a nearby stack of timber. "Before starting a fire, you must collect the right wood, as different woods burn differently." He placed the branch on the campfire in front of him. "Ash is the best-burning wood. It has both flame and heat and will burn when green. This"—he held up another log—"is birch, which has a nice smell and gives good heat, but it burns quickly." One by one, he piled pieces of wood atop the fire. "Cedar has lots of crackle and snap, with little flame but much heat, and the scent is pleasant. Oak is sparse in flame with acrid smoke but is excellent for heat. It burns slowly and steadily and is your best choice for a cooking fire. Pine gives off a cheerful blue flame, but because of the resin, it tends to pop."

Michael's friendly, knowledgeable demeanor captured his audience. His coal-black hair and beard and hazel eyes captivated Anne more.

A picture came to mind of Michael out in a forest, axe in hand, felling a tall tree. Shirtless. His arm muscles bulging.

An odd sensation roiled in her stomach. She swallowed hard.

What a ninnyhammer I am.

She banished the vision from her mind and hurried back to the wagon. Inside, she opened one of the chests and removed one of David's shirts. She settled on the backboard and enjoyed the breeze while she darned the tear in the sleeve.

At noon, she and Gail and William spread a blanket next to their wagon and greeted two maids from the inn. One toted a picnic lunch, and the other carried Keith in one arm and held David's hand with the other as he walked beside her. After making their deliveries, the women left, promising to return in an hour. Following the meal, William wandered across the field to rejoin the firearms practice, and Gail stretched out on her side on the blanket. Anne allowed the boys to explore the wagon. When they tired of climbing on the boxes inside, they cuddled next to their mother to nap.

Lying on the coverlet propped on her elbows, Anne grew drowsy...until she spotted the maids racing toward her. The terror on their faces made her stomach muscles clench.

My dear Lord, what could be so terrible?

~

Four wagons down from the Forbes, Michael finished off a fried chicken leg and wiped his hands on a cloth. The Smythes and the Tanners had invited him, Megan, and Amelia to share their lunch. They were congenial people, and he looked forward to getting to know them. Wishing the Forbes had been invited, he glanced their way.

Anne jumped up from their picnic blanket, shielded her eyes with her hand, and searched across the field. Standing with the maids who were now sobbing, she pressed a hand to her heart.

"Something is amiss," he said to the others and raced to Anne's side. "What is it, Anne?"

Her face, usually so calm and in control, was tense with anxiety. "We must find the wagon master."

He clasped her forearm. How hard she trembled. "Tell me."

Her soft brown eyes locked with his. Fear dilated her pupils, turning them dark-chocolate brown. "Smallpox...the maids... they say smallpox is raging through the city." She gripped his sleeve. "What should we do, Michael?"

His heart hammered. "I cannot say I'm not worried. As a young man, I survived the pox and will never forget what a horrible time that was."

Anne shook even more, but he resisted the urge to gather her into his arms. "Stay here. I'll find Mr. Cooper, and we'll make a plan."

Within minutes, Mr. Cooper and the scout had assembled all the wagoners around Anne and her family. William, holding Keith in his arms, clutched Gail to his side with David huddled into his mother's petticoats.

"Ladies..." Mr. Cooper addressed the maids. "Now that you've calmed down enough to speak, please, tell us what you heard."

The tiny older woman wrung her hands. "Word is, there's smallpox and it's spreading fast. The sheriff sent out constables and the volunteer night watchmen to order us to stay in our homes."

Several women cried out, and others mumbled among themselves.

The maid pressed her hands to her pale, wrinkled face. "Saints preserve us. They are blocking the streets so that no one can enter or leave the city. People are scurrying about in a panic."

The younger woman started whimpering and grabbed the other's arm. "Come, Hazel. I'm so scared. I ain't never had the pox. We must get back."

The frightened women skittered away, and Michael lifted up a silent prayer for them and for the people trapped in the city.

"All right." Mr. Cooper stood ramrod stiff. "Many of you camped in your tents the past couple of days until the wagons arrived. Did any of you go into town?"

Most of the wagoners looked at each other and shook their heads. Only Michael and William raised their hands.

Michael lowered his hand. "Both our parties lodged in inns at the edge of the city the past two days."

"The rest of us pretty much all remained here since our ships landed." Mr. Smythe frowned at his wife. "Though there was some sickness aboard."

Mrs. Smythe whimpered and gripped her husband's hand.

"Mr. Forbes and Mr. Harrigan, I'm making a serious decision...which some might call unwise...but you have my permission to fetch your belongings. But you mustn't venture anywhere else. Is that clear?"

"It is." Michael and William spoke the words together.

Mr. Cooper rested an arm on the pistol secured in his belt. "No one...and I mean no one else...may leave this area."

"But," said Mr. Waters, a farmer whose face was tanned and wrinkled from many hours in the sun, "I'd planned to order corn and vegetable seeds before departing."

The wagon master grimaced. "If anyone leaves other than Mr. Harrigan or Mr. Forbes, you will not be allowed to come back in."

Mr. Waters's shoulders slumped.

"Don't be disheartened, sir." Mr. Cooper's expression softened. "Once we are on the trail, we will stop by settlements where you can purchase seeds. Speaking of the trail, everyone should be prepared to leave at dawn. That means horses harnessed, livestock gathered, and wagons in place according to your numbers."

Michael frowned. "Will we be allowed to leave?"

The scout stepped forward. "I'll check with the constables. We have been fairly isolated here on the edge of town. Just over there"—he motioned to the forest—"is the entrance to the trail. The authorities may not see a problem with our going. May even be relieved."

"Let's go, William," Michael said. "The sooner we get our things and get back, the better."

Anne moved close to her brother. "We both had the pox when we were children. What about Gail?"

"No. She's in danger." He looked down at David fidgeting beside him and Keith, sleepy-eyed in his mother's arms. He swallowed so hard, his Adam's apple bobbed.

William's pale face and the haunted expression in his eyes panged Michael's heart. He clapped him on his shoulder. "We mustn't be afraid or discouraged, William. Our Lord is with us wherever we go."

Anne glanced up at Michael with the same look of trust she had given him when they first met. "Keep each other safe," she said in a lowered voice. "Frightened people do strange things."

Who would keep Anne safe?

It took an hour for Michael and William to find a livery stable and a driver willing to transport their belongings. It cost a small fortune. Though Michael could well afford it, William insisted on sharing his part. Another hour passed as they gathered chests and luggage from their rooms. Their driver refused to budge from the wagon. He covered his face with a kerchief and kept a beady eye on the people hurrying past.

When they had loaded the back, the driver slapped the reins to pull away from the inn, but a man ran in front of them frantically waving his arms.

"Where'd you get this?" he demanded. Despite his rough behavior, their accoster wore a gentleman's attire.

Michael, seated next to the driver, reached for the pistol secured in his belt. He cast a warning glance at William, sitting atop one of the chests.

"Are you mad, running in front of me like that?" the driver shouted.

The man grabbed the harness of one of the horses. "I want to know where you got the wagon."

"From the livery down the street. I'll be back there in an hour." The driver brandished his whip. "But for right now, get out of my way...or else."

Though the man stepped back, Michael kept his hand on his weapon. They made their way toward the city limits and past knots of people moving furtively up and down the street. Several men, eyeing them closely, crossed the road in front of them but did not approach.

Michael pulled his pistol from his belt and laid it on his lap. "We must keep at the ready."

William nodded

When they reached the campsite, William jumped down and ran straight into his wife's arms.

"Oh, my dearest one." Tears spilled down Gail's face as she kissed his eyelids and then his lips. "It is quite wonderful to see you. I have imagined all manner of things happening to you. Can we make a pact not to be parted again?"

A deep yearning flowed through Michael. How splendid to be greeted in such a manner.

Anne paused nearby, her arms twined about her waist. The expression on her face mirrored his thoughts.

*a*fter supper, the wagoners gathered around Mr. Cooper in the center of the campsite. Anne and William stood among them. Gail remained at their wagon with the boys. The tension in the air was palpable.

"I've brought us together to let you know we have been given permission to leave tomorrow at dawn."

"Good," yelled Mr. Johnson. "Would we could leave tonight."

Many in the crowd mumbled their agreement.

"I know how anxious you must be, but you signed a contract. And part of that is your agreement to follow my orders. So...you will each position your wagon in line tomorrow morning per your wagon number." Mr. Cooper held out his arms. "Any more questions?" He removed his hat. "No? Then I ask that we bow our heads and beseech the Almighty for a safe journey."

At the end of his prayer, many of the group echoed a fervent *amen* before disbursing.

The wagon master approached Anne as she tucked David and Keith under the covers of the pallet she had spread beneath their wagon. Gail and William, huddled together at the campfire, would join them soon. She would sleep on a pallet sheltered from the elements by a canopy stretched out from the wagon bed.

"May I have a moment of your time, Miss Forbes?" He motioned away from the wagon.

"Certainly."

The boys already slept soundly. Whatever could he want?

She followed him until he stopped after a few yards. "I understand from your brother that you had experience with smallpox."

Anne pursed her lips. "About five years ago, our village in Scotland suffered a smallpox epidemic. Because I had the disease as a child and couldn't succumb to it again, I...and others...helped our doctor treat the sick."

"I've some knowledge of the disease...but no experience. What more can you tell me about the sickness so I'm prepared?"

"I remember there being three kinds. The one that lasted only a few days. The one that was a bit harsher. And the one that was fatal." Anne slipped her hands into her apron pockets. "There was no known treatment. We simply tried to make people as comfortable as we could while their bodies did the work."

His features softened. "Isn't it amazing how God designed our bodies to heal themselves?"

"Truly."

He removed his hat and ran a kerchief around its sweaty band. "Anything else I should know?"

"Once the symptoms show, it's vital to keep the sick separated from the well." Anne breathed deeply. "That's a difficult task...keeping loved ones apart. Especially mothers from their children."

He stared directly into Anne's eyes, and she braced herself, certain of his next words.

"You will help, should the need arise?"

"I will."

"Thank you. I don't know you well, Miss Forbes, but I feel I can rely on you. Let's hope we don't need your help."

"One more thing, Mr. Cooper. If no one has fallen ill within the next twelve days, we can be fairly certain we will not fall prey to the 'speckled monster.'"

Anne hoped that would be the case. The alternative was too awful to imagine.

Please, Lord, spare us.

CHAPTER 4

*A*ccording to plan, at dawn, they left the chaos of the city without incident. The scout guided them out of the clearing and onto a road that meandered through a dense forest. A morning mist dampened the hair on Anne's arms and hung over the thick underbrush like a shroud.

Walking alongside their wagon, the last in line, Anne's heart raced, and she breathed deeply. Caught up in the eagerness of the others, she did not look back once at the city. The future held her thoughts.

What would the next three months bring as they trekked the three hundred miles to their destination in the South Carolina colony? She would not allow the looming threat of sickness to spoil her excitement.

Traversing the well-trodden path went smoothly. A spirit of congeniality was already forming among the traveling companions. The newness of sleeping on the ground under the stars and cooking over a campfire, even in the sweltering heat, proved exhilarating for Anne.

Not so for Gail. She found much to complain about over the

next two days. The smoke irritated her eyes. The morning dew dampened the coverlets. The food tasted strange. Mosquitos tormented the boys. Strange creatures lurked from every direction.

Anne prayed that her sister-in-law would quickly adapt and learn to enjoy the adventure. William, caught up in the same contagious enthusiasm as Anne, clearly only half listened to Gail's harangues. He grinned and winked often.

Her love for her brother magnified. How wonderful to share this adventure with a kindred spirit.

The third day of the journey, Anne walked alongside their wagon holding onto David's hand. Keeping him in check proved more difficult than she had imagined, as the young lad took great delight in his surroundings. Everything captured his interest, including a black snake that slithered across their path. Anne lifted praise to the heavens that Gail had not seen it.

During their noon break, while many wagoners napped, Anne decided to seek out the patch of blackberries she had spotted on the trail outside the clearing where they had circled the wagons. Gail lay on a pallet under the wagon keeping David cool with her fan. William visited Mr. Johnson, getting a shoe repaired and chatting with a group of men gathered there.

Anne adjusted the length of cloth wound across her shoulder and wrapped around her waist which held Keith tucked against her midriff. She slowly leaned down and picked up her leather gloves and a woven basket.

"Be careful, Anne," Gail whispered, trying not to wake her sons. "And don't forget your hat."

Anne frowned at her dreaded hat she had thrown onto her pallet. The desire to resist propriety, to loosen her hair and let the wind flow through it, tempted her. If she already thought such things after only a few days in the wilderness, next, would she go barefoot? Would she alter into some sort of feral being by the end of their journey? Heady thoughts for a twenty-eight-year-old spinster seamstress. She chuckled.

She lay the basket on the ground and tossed her gloves into it. She plopped her hat on her head and tied the ribbons at the back of her neck. "We'll be fine. It's not that far. I'll still be able to see the wagons."

On her way out of the campsite, Anne waved at the Smythes, who sat in the shade of a giant oak seeking respite from the blistering sun. The girls, Elspeth and Charlotte, hurried to her.

"Where you goin', Miss Forbes?" asked Charlotte, the older of the two.

"Blackberry picking. Would you like to come with me?" she asked, keeping her voice low.

Elspeth twirled around. "Oh yes! I should like that."

"Not too loud, Elspeth. Keith is falling asleep." Anne rubbed her fingers across Keith's back.

Charlotte tiptoed close and peeked into the wrap. "Isn't he sweet?"

"You must ask your parents if you may go with me. If they say yes, you'll have to wear gloves to protect your hands from the thorns."

She waited while the girls got permission from their parents, gathered some gloves, and hurried back. Charlotte took the basket from Anne as they exited the clearing. As soon as they stepped back onto the trail, they found the blackberry patch a short distance away, where she and the girls slipped on their gloves.

"There are so many, I don't know where to start," Elspeth exclaimed and popped a handful in her mouth. "Umm. So good."

Charlotte ate a few berries and wiped purple juice from the corners of her mouth. "They are delicious. Back home near our tenant farm in England, we didn't usually pick until late July or August."

"Yes, I was surprised to find so many ripe berries, but the wagon master mentioned that wild berries ripen here as early as May sometimes. He also warned that snakes like the berries, too, so we must be cautious."

Anne hated sharing the last information, but this was the wilderness, and everyone, including children, had to learn about its dangers.

Her mouth watered, and she could not resist sampling the plump, juicy berries any more than the children could. The sudden sweetness on her tongue made her jaws ache for a moment. She mentally listed the ingredients necessary for a cobbler. Yes, she had them all. Her family would enjoy a cobbler this very night.

"Ouch!" Elspeth yelped and yanked a branch that clung to her petticoats. "Why does something so delicious have to have stickers?"

Her sister gingerly helped her free of the prickly branch, trying hard not to tear the cloth. "Sometimes things are more valuable if they are difficult to get."

What an impressive person. Charlotte was one of those rare young people, an old soul, mature beyond her years.

"How do you both feel, leaving your home and coming to a strange place?" Anne asked.

"Elspeth and I were sad at first. But we both see it now as a grand adventure. The talk about all the criminals in Georgia is a bit frightening, though." The girls nodded to each other.

"We miss our friends." Elspeth dropped a handful of berries into the basket. "But Ma says we can make new ones in Georgia. And if we don't, we always have each other."

"I understand. My brother, Mr. Forbes, and I have always been close. I'm happy that we can share our grand adventure together."

They spent the latter part of an hour silently enjoying the breezes that whipped down the trail and across the thicket. As they tossed the last berries into the basket, Keith started to squirm. Anne loosened the boy from the binding cloth and slid him up close to her shoulder, enjoying the feel of his soft, plump little legs on her arms. He yawned, stretched, and whimpered.

"We must get back, girls. Keith will be hungry."

Charlotte picked up the basket. "Thank you for inviting us, Miss Forbes."

Anne led the way back to the campsite. "It was my pleasure. You'll need to bring me a container so we can share."

When they reached the Smythes' wagon, Charlotte grabbed a bucket and started dumping the berries from the basket. "Is that too much?"

Anne slid Keith onto her hip. "Take more. About half will be fine."

Once the division of berries was complete, Anne picked up the basket, waved to the Smythes, and crossed the clearing to their wagon, where she found Gail fast asleep. She looked for David. He was not there.

"Gail!" she shouted. "Where is David?"

Gail sat up groggy and confused. "What do you mean? He's right..." She felt the covers and scooted out from under the wagon. "Is William here? Maybe he has him."

William, still conversing with Mr. Johnson and several other men including Michael, glanced her way.

Panic roiled in Anne's stomach. Where was David? Had he wandered off into the woods? She must stay calm.

She held Keith out to Gail. "Here, you take him."

She tossed the toddler into her sister-in-law's arms, and running faster than she had ever moved in her life, she almost collided with her brother now headed to their wagon.

Michael, who accompanied William, gripped her forearm to steady her. "Whoa, Anne. What's amiss?"

"It's...it's David." She jerked William's shirtsleeve. "We can't find him."

The color flooded from her brother's face. "What?"

"Let's all go," Michael ordered.

The group—William, Mr. Johnson, and the Daniels brothers—ran to the wagon, where Gail clutched Keith and sobbed uncontrollably.

She looked up at her husband with eyes fraught with anxiety and fear. "I-I fell asleep. He was asleep too. He can't have gone far."

"All right." Michael glanced around the campsite. "Let's gather everyone and start searching."

All the wagoners quickly surrounded Michael. Anne's pulse raced so fast, she could hardly breathe. *Hurry, hurry.* She wanted with every part of her to start looking for her darling nephew.

Was he scared? Was he hurt? *Oh, please, Lord, have mercy on us. Please, help us to find David.*

Michael stiffened his spine. "The wagon master and the scout have gone ahead on the trail, so I'll take charge. Everyone fan out at the back of the wagon. Stay no more than ten feet apart. We don't want anyone getting lost."

"How far can a little boy go in just a few minutes?" asked Megan, standing beside Amelia.

"He's...he's only four," Anne stammered. "He can't have gone far."

"The creek! What if he went to the creek?" Gail called from the wagon.

Anne took off running. When she reached the creek only a few yards from the clearing, she frantically scrambled up and down the banks. Michael followed closely.

Her heart hammered against her ribcage. "David isn't here. Neither in the water nor in the woods nearby."

"We'll find him, Anne." He touched his fingertips to the small of her back and guided her back toward the clearing.

They joined the men and women now combing the forest around the back of the wagons. Every few steps garnered a new prayer. Over and over, Anne beseeched the Lord for His grace.

Soon they had covered an area much larger than David could have traveled in twice the time. Discouraged, they returned to the terrified parents.

The pain in her brother's eyes raked across Anne's heart, and she threw her arms around him.

"My little boy. My little boy." He kept repeating the words, his voice raspy.

She must not cry. She must not lose control.

She let go of William and faced Michael. "What next?"

Surely, he had answers...a plan. Where would he lead them? She had known Michael for only a short time. What about him gave her such faith in him?

He closed his eyes and stood still. He was praying. That gesture answered her question. He was a man of God and sought His guidance. When she clasped his hand and began to pray with him, the others bowed their heads.

Moments later, Michael raised his head and scanned the campsite. "We assumed he walked away from the back of the wagon. He could have backtracked. We must search in the other direction."

"But, surely, if he crossed inside the circle, someone would have seen him." Anne reluctantly let go of Michael's hand. "I would have seen him when I came back from picking blackberries."

Had only a few minutes passed since that serene time?

Michael swept his arm over the clearing. "Let's spread out.

Scour the camp. Consider anywhere a little boy might be enticed to go."

Anne searched around the wagon next to theirs, then the next, and the next. She made the rounds, joining others lifting up piles of clothes, rummaging underneath pallets, and over-turning boxes. Wary, she walked near the draft horses tethered outside the circle. She quickly shut out of her mind the picture of David making his way among the deadly hooves. Her prayers had dwindled from full sentences to repeating *please, please, please.*

Just as her spirits plummeted to their lowest, someone yelled, "Halleluiah! Thank the Lord!"

She stumbled away from the horses and raced across the clearing to catch Michael coming away from the Tanners' wagon with David on his shoulders.

Relief threatened to buckle her knees.

Her nephew's spindly legs dangled on either side of Michael's head. He clamped his hands around his rescuer's thick black beard, reminding her of the first time she encoun-tered Michael. David giggled, thoroughly enjoying the ride. His parents, with Gail holding tightly to Keith, reached their son first and pulled him into their arms, laughing and crying at the same time.

"According to David, he went to visit the goats. He wanted to see where his milk came from." Michael grinned. "He fell sound asleep and didn't hear us calling."

Impulsively, Anne hugged Michael. His physique was so brawny, her arms did not fit around his waist. Though it felt quite pleasant, she quickly stepped away, avoiding eye contact.

"Praise the Lord," Mr. Johnson yelled.

"Praise Him, indeed." Mr. Smythe laughed and squeezed his wife and daughters to him.

The elated wagoners clapped their hands and slapped each

other's backs. Several had tears in their eyes. The near tragedy had brought them together as friends...family. What a blessing.

Joy and unbelievable happiness and relief took turns racing through Anne as she gathered her little family close. She lifted a quick prayer of thanksgiving. Her evening prayers would take much longer. She caught Michael's attention. Once again, he had come to her family's rescue. She mouthed the words, *thank you*. He smiled and pointed to the sky.

What an exceptional person. She yearned to know more about him. Maybe they would become friends.

Did she dare contemplate a closer relationship?

CHAPTER 5

*A*t dawn, a week to the day of their departure from Philadelphia, Anne awoke to the loud wails of Mrs. Smythe, which echoed through the camp.

"The pox!" the woman shouted. "My daughters! Dear Lord in heaven be with us."

Anne shoved open her dew-dampened covers and crawled out of her makeshift tent. She wrapped a shawl over her stays and the top of her shift and tied it in a knot at her back, then straightened her rumpled petticoats that clung to her legs.

She bent down to check on her family bedded beneath the wagon. William sat up so fast, he almost slammed his head against the wagon bed. David, sitting between his parents, started to whimper. His brother remained curled in a ball next to his mother.

"What's happening, Anne?" Gail asked in a voice groggy from sleep.

Truth stated calmly served best. "The worst possible thing. I believe the Smythe girls have smallpox."

Gail scooped up Keith and cuddled him on her lap. "What do we do?"

"You remain here. Let me find if my suspicions are correct."

The Smythes camped four wagons away. On her way, she passed Megan and Amelia, dressed in their nightclothes, clinging to one another. By the time Anne arrived, a small crowd had gathered, including Michael and Mr. Cooper. Michael locked eyes with her, and the dread in them confirmed her conclusions.

Mr. Cooper's mouth and eyes were downturned. "Seems I'll need your help, Miss Forbes."

"You have it, Mr. Cooper."

"And mine." Michael regarded Anne's face and the braid draped over her shoulder. "What do you need?"

His scrutiny made her conscious of her disheveled appearance and her bare toes poking out from under her hem. Silly woman. Now was not the time to consider such trivialities.

"First, we must move these people away from here and order everyone to stay near their wagons and apart from one another. Then find out who has had the pox and would be willing to help if others get sick."

Which they most assuredly would. What of her sister-in-law and nephews?

"I'll do that," said Mr. Cooper. "Our scout should be returning soon and can help also." He immediately started wrangling the onlookers, encouraging them to return to their wagons.

Anne faced Michael, noticing for the first time that he was barefooted and wore only breeches and a shirt that billowed to his knees. His coal-black curly hair fell loosely to his neck. Appealing.

A thought struck her. "Didn't you mention that you have had smallpox?"

He ran a finger across a tiny circular scar on his right temple. "I have."

She blew out a big breath. "I need to return to my family

and inform them of what's happening. If you would join me there, Michael?"

"I will. Once I've calmed Megan and Amelia. I left them in a state."

They passed the Tanner wagon where Eleanor glanced up from pouring her husband a cup of coffee, grimaced, and shook her head.

"The situation is dire, is it not?" Michael asked.

"It most likely will get worse before it gets better."

"My mind is awash with a thousand thoughts, as I am sure is yours." He stopped. "One thought overrides all. That is the promise that we can do all things through Christ who strengthens us. In Him, we can persevere and be content amidst all the turmoil."

"Thank you for those words. I have a feeling I'll need to lean on them in the coming days."

"Mr. Cooper has great faith in you, but it will be an enormous burden."

She rubbed her fingertips across her forehead. "I've had experience, but I'm sure there are others here willing to come forward and shoulder the burden with me."

He glanced at Megan and Amelia huddled beside their wagon. "Be assured, Anne, I consider myself among those. Let me calm these two, and I'll be with you soon."

He waved, and she continued on to her wagon where she quickly dressed.

William and Gail waited by the wagon with the boys. When Anne neared, David ran to her and hugged her leg.

"What news?" her brother asked.

"It's as I feared. The Smythe girls have smallpox. I am to help."

William blanched. "I'd offer to assist, but I simply cannot. I have my wife and boys to consider. They're in grave danger."

"I don't expect anything else of you." She rumpled David's

thick head of hair, the same sable brown as his father's. "There are others, I'm sure, who have had the pox and will volunteer. Besides, I can do what I have to do better if I know the four of you are safe."

He shook his head, his expression grim.

She headed for the back of the wagon. "I must gather some of my clothes and personal things, as I'll be sequestered."

"Must you accept this, Anne?" Gail rested her hands on Anne's shoulders. "I've never spoken of this, but I do realize how much you do for us."

Anne started to respond. "I—"

"Please, hear me out." Gail cupped Anne's cheek. "You're as much a part of this family as any of us. But in my selfishness, I have allowed you to take on responsibilities that should have been mine. And so has William."

Tears welled in Anne's eyes. "I do so willingly. Out of love."

"We know. You're a strong, reliable, organized, and capable person with a huge heart. That's why I am asking you, please, don't assume the majority of this. Take care of yourself. Rest, eat, and sleep as you should."

Unable to respond due to the lump in her throat, Anne embraced her sister-in-law. She grabbed a coverlet, climbed into the wagon, and sorted through her trunk. Once she had rolled her belongings into the cover, Michael appeared at the back of the wagon and took the bundle from her.

He held out his arms. "May I assist you?"

She had dismounted the wagon many times on her own. He had helped her once before, and his closeness had stirred her. Then there was the way he felt when she hugged him. She could not resist the chance to experience his nearness again and allowed him to clasp her waist. With little effort, he lifted her from the backboard and placed her feet gently on the ground. His chest was solid...warm. With her hands on his shoulders, Anne relished the few moments he encircled her in his strong embrace.

David released his father's hand to grab a tiny fistful of her skirts.

She knelt down and tucked a curl behind his ear. "Auntie Anne has to leave for a while, but I won't be far away. You may even see me. And when you do, I'll wave and call out. But, as your mommy will explain, I may not hold you and your brother for a while."

David's bottom lip quivered. "You will not sing us to sleep anymore?"

The sadness in the little one's eyes made Anne's heart ache. Michael's steady hand on her shoulder kept her from giving in to her despondency. "Only for a few days. I promise, I'll sing for you then."

Keeping a tight rein on her emotions, Anne hurried away, resisting the terrible urge to look back. When she and Michael stopped at the opening of the wagon circle, she sucked in a deep breath.

Michael's hazel eyes held deep sympathy. "That was difficult, I know."

"Not near as difficult as what lies ahead." She squared her shoulders. "So let's begin."

Mr. Cooper and Mr. Sanders strode across the campsite and joined them.

"We must designate an area for our shelter." She pointed to a clearing beside the river that flowed alongside the camp. "There is a good place. We need a type of fence...maybe rope... to provide a boundary. We need a canopy stretched over the area. A shelter from the rain and sun." Her mind raced as she ticked off her list on her fingers. "Barrels and buckets for a steady supply of hot and cold water. And a fire with lots of firewood."

Mr. Cooper motioned to Mr. Waters on the other side of the encampment. "I'll take care of the barrels and buckets."

"And I'll make a rope boundary and find a canopy. Maybe one of the wagon bonnets," offered the scout.

Michael crossed his arms over his chest. "I'll handle the fire and wood."

"My first task will be to bring the Smythe girls to the clearing." Anne started to move away but stopped when Michael held up his hand.

"Before we separate, might we pray together?" he asked.

Michael, the wagon master, and the scout removed their hats, and Anne bowed her head while Michael offered a prayer for strength, wisdom, and God's presence in the coming days. After fervent *amens*, they each went about their designated tasks.

Anne approached the Smythes' wagon. The parents hovered over their girls, who were bundled up lying on their bedding, shaking from head to toe.

Anne had had several occasions, including blackberry picking, to become acquainted with the daughters. Charlotte, twelve and mature for her age, had a serious disposition and talked sparsely. Elspeth at nine was livelier than her sister.

She studied their mother's anxious pallor. "Hannah, this is frightening, I know. I'm not a doctor, but I had some experience with smallpox in my village in Scotland five years ago. For that reason, Mr. Cooper asked if I would organize caring for the sick." Anne bent down next to the girls. "I'm so very sorry you are ill. May I see your hands?"

Charlotte reached out first. Anne studied her palms and then Elspeth's. The telltale rash had spread quickly and covered their skin.

"The rash is on your feet also?"

The girls nodded.

Hannah wrung her hands. Panic filled her eyes. "I feared this would happen. Some people on our passage from England were sick, but they were in the hold, and we were never told what it was. In the passenger cabins, we were packed together with hardly room to breathe. It's a wonder we didn't all get sick."

That sickness had been aboard their ship bothered Anne. How far would the pox spread in the city? She had enough to worry about and needed to concentrate on taking care of the girls.

"Because we must keep the sick away from the well, we have set aside an area"—she motioned to the spot by the river—"over there where we will tend to them. Are you prepared for the girls to come with me?"

"We are." Herald reached down to help Elspeth to her feet. "But we are coming with you."

Anne's heart sank. How could she convince them to leave their children in someone else's care? "But—"

"Don't worry, Miss Forbes, my wife and I had smallpox as children."

Herald's words lifted the concerns that weighed like a brick upon her chest. She would have support. He threw the pallet covers over his shoulder and put an arm around his younger daughter.

Elspeth, whose face had grown alarmingly pale, moaned and swayed. "Oh, Papa, I'm dizzy and I may vomit."

Herald clasped her closer. "Papa's here, little one."

Hannah helped Charlotte to stand, and Anne secured a blanket around the girl's shoulders. The heat from her fever raged through the cloth as her mother and Anne supported her between them. Once they reached the shelter, Anne and the Smythes spread out covers on the ground and helped the girls lie down. Mr. Sanford had already strung ropes on three sides of the boundary with an opening in the fourth. As he and Herald attached the corners of a wagon canvas with ropes to nearby trees, Michael, axe in hand, strode across the clearing to assist. The three of them made quick work of securing a canopy overhead, blocking out the midmorning sun. Mr. Cooper and Paul Waters rolled barrels into one corner of the area, followed by Paul's wife, Winnet, carrying buckets.

"Where do you want these, Anne?" Winnet asked.

During the past few days, in the evenings when the wagoners had gathered after supper, Anne had become friends with the slender yet sturdy woman the same age as Anne. Her face and arms were tanned and covered with freckles from growing corn on their tenant farm in England.

"Let's set them beside the water barrels for the time being."

Winnet put the buckets down and brushed her hands on her skirts. "'Case you're worrying, Paul and I had cowpox a few years back, so we ain't concerned about the pox. Eleanor Tanner and her husband don't have a concern either. Eleanor, Molly Hudson, and I will cook meals for you and your volunteers. When the time is right, we'll make chicken and beef broth for those that can tolerate it."

Overcome with gratitude, Anne reached out and clasped the woman to her. "You are a godsend."

By late afternoon, the wagoners had donated a table and two chairs, coffee pots and cups, extra covers, and washing cloths made from torn linens.

Sitting at the table, Hannah helped Anne sort through the herbs and remedies offered by the women who had emptied their medicine chests.

Hannah picked up a palm-sized jar with a cork stopper. "This is calamine powder. We mix it with water to make a paste for the itching."

Anne held the clay pot. "We'll need this in a couple of days when the spots form."

Picking up the items one by one, Hannah explained, "We

have several ingredients for teas. Boneset and cinchona bark for fever. Chamomile for nausea and sleep."

Anne placed the items on a tin plate. "I have black willow twigs. My mother used to boil them into a tea to ease my father's rheumatism. It will help with the back pain and soreness."

Melancholy washed over Anne as she thought of her parents. Years had passed since their deaths, almost erasing any recollection of their faces. Since then, William had acted as her only parent. She could not have desired a better one.

A movement near the river caught her eye. Michael had pulled off his shirt and was swinging an axe, cutting a fallen tree into kindling. Sweat glistened on his shoulders and accentuated his taut stomach muscles. He leaned the axe against his leg, grabbed his shirt, and rubbed it across his forehead and face and then his chest with the dark hairs that tapered into a faint line that disappeared into his breeches waistband. Captivating. A truly wonderfully made man.

The scene bore an uncanny resemblance to the vision she once had of him. She scrubbed the goosebumps on her arms. Before she could drag her attention away, Amelia ran up to him and gripped his forearm, shaking and sobbing uncontrollably.

Michael threw on his shirt and ran toward the circled wagons. In anticipation, Anne moved to the front of the rope barrier. Minutes later, Michael appeared carrying Megan, whose body lay limp in his arms. An obviously distraught Amelia followed him, tears flowing down her face. Michael soon moved close enough for Anne to see the rash on Megan's forehead. Anne and he stared at one another. His teeth clenched so hard, the muscles in his cheeks twitched.

"Bring Megan over here," Anne instructed.

Amelia's eyes shone overly bright.

"Not one step closer, Amelia. You may not come in here."

"But what am I to do? With Michael and Megan here, I shall be alone." She pressed both hands to her heart.

"You must return to your wagon."

The woman's pitiful state tugged at Anne's heart. She was, after all, alone in an unknown land, surrounded by strangers, and her best friend had fallen ill.

"We'll care for Megan the best we know how, and we will inform you about her as often as we are able. I'm certain some of the others, possibly the Tanners or the Waters, will share a meal with you."

Dejected, her shoulders slumping, Amelia walked away.

"Wait." Anne said. "Have you had the pox?"

"No, I have not," she replied over her shoulder and continued on.

Anne lowered her head. Would they have another patient soon?

After she and Hannah settled Megan on a pallet in line with Elspeth and Charlotte, Anne joined Michael near the front of the enclosure.

"Megan concerns me. Her fever is much higher than it should be, and the rash has covered much of her body. We must watch her closely."

Michael glanced at Megan and then looked down at Anne. "She's in good hands." He gazed at the sky that was turning a soft pink. "Night is falling. I'll bring the wood and start a fire."

The fire had barely begun to crackle when Ezra and Claire Banks, holding onto one another for support, staggered into the shelter. Mark and Matilda Daniels stumbled after them, followed by Oliver Tanner, who carried a lethargic Amelia in his arms and handed her over to Michael.

Anne raised her eyes to the heavens and beseeched the Lord for His mercy. They all would need it in the coming days.

I can do all things...

CHAPTER 6

$\mathcal{A}$s the morning rays of the sun filtered through the forest and burned away the mist that hung in the air, Michael dropped an armload of logs on the ground and tossed a couple of them onto the shelter fire. He added more river rocks to the circle around the flames and placed a coffeepot atop one of them. He would make sure Anne drank a cup.

Next to the rope boundary, Anne sat on her knees bending over Amelia, pressing a cool cloth to her forehead and consoling her to stop crying. The Smythes tried to coax their daughters to sip some cinchona bark tea. The Danielses and the Bankses lay on their bedding, awake but listless.

Two days had passed since their terrible ordeal began. Michael's admiration for Anne grew with each passing hour. A born leader, she handled each obstacle with good sense, grace, and compassion. But the burden wore on her. Her face was pale, and light-blue circles colored the skin under her soft-brown eyes.

He had accomplished what he could to make things easier for her—keeping the fire going, making sure the hot water was plentiful, and either boiling or disposing of the soiled rags. He had even strung up a lumberman's hammock to keep her off the ground when she managed to rest. He had also hung a cover from the canopy to provide a privacy screen for her and the other women as they slept. When the ladies brought food, he persuaded her to sit with him at the table and eat.

He walked over to Amelia's pallet and helped Anne to stand. She leaned heavily on his arm.

"There are eight now," she said, scanning the shelter. "The sisters are faring well. As are the Danielses and the Bankses. And Amelia." She glanced at Megan and whispered, "I fear for your sister-in-law."

Before Michael could respond, William, holding his boys in each arm, trudged toward the shelter. Gail stumbled behind him, grasping the waist of his breeches for support. Tears flowed down William's face.

A staggering dread flowed through Michael, and he reached out and took Anne by her shoulders. "Brace yourself, Anne."

She spun around, and her knees buckled. She would have fallen if it were not for Michael leaning her back against him.

"No-o-o! No! No!" She ran and pulled David from her brother's arms.

Michael held Gail's forearm and circled her waist with his other arm. Her body was on fire, and a rash spread across her forehead. Would the pox take her? Ravage her beautiful skin? "Come with me, Gail. We'll make a place for you to lie down with your boys."

Kneeling on the pallet she had laid on the ground, Anne pulled up David's nightgown.

"Auntie Anne, I am hot."

"We'll get you better soon, dear one." She barely choked out the words.

Michael longed to hold her, comfort her.

She examined David's body from head to toe. She did the

same for Keith, who lay unresponsive next to his mother. She pressed her hands to her face as she looked up at the sky.

"William, we must...*must*...make the boys drink. Water... tea...coffee. It doesn't matter." Her bottom lip trembled. "It's vital. Do you understand?"

The panic in Anne's voice and the dread in her eyes caused Michael to fear the worst.

~

*T*he following two days, the disease continued its dreadful progress from one stage to another. Michael felt trapped in a living nightmare.

The wagon master and the scout stayed away, performing their duties, attending to the other wagoners, the draft horses, and the livestock, and making sure provisions remained plentiful. To lighten Anne's burden and free her to concentrate on her family, Eleanor Tanner and Molly Hudson assumed the responsibility of tending to the other patients.

Michael sat at the table, resting his eyes and remaining close, at the ready, to do whatever necessary.

Eleanor approached Anne as she pressed a cool cloth down Gail's arms. "What else can we do?"

Anne dipped the cloth in the bucket of water beside her and wrung it out. "The lesions will be forming soon. If you would, start adding water to the calamine powder and make a paste." She paused. "And find some gloves. Once the itching starts, it's unbearable. Scratching the spots will cause infection and scarring."

"I'll check with the other ladies and fetch some gloves." Eleanor scrubbed her hands down her arms. "I don't think I'll ever forget the horrible itching. I had spots on my tongue, my eyelids, and in my ears."

Eleanor's descriptions brought back memories to Michael

of his own experience with smallpox. He left the table and stood beside Megan as she lay on her pallet shivering uncontrollably.

Anne joined him. Her face was drained of color, deep lines furrowed her brow, and her usually bright eyes were dull. Blood, mucus, coffee, and other stains spattered her apron. Perspiration stained the underarms of her bodice, and wisps of sweat-dampened curls framed her face. He had never admired her more.

She spoke to him in a low voice. "Her response to the illness isn't like the others. I fear for her, Michael. The whites of her eyes are bloody red and may turn black."

Michael gasped.

Anne stared off into the forest, rose up on her tiptoes, and whispered in his ear, "And...she has stopped making water. You must prepare yourself."

For Megan's death? How could he prepare himself for that? What of his brother?

Michael found it difficult to swallow and bent down next to Megan. Her chest barely rose with her labored breaths. Her depleted state unsettled him. She opened her eyes and reached for his hand.

"I'm sorry, Michael." She barely croaked the words. "Tell Cal...tell Cal I did love him. I'm sorry I wasn't a better wife."

Michael studied her once-lovely face now bloated and ravaged by rash, and he regretted every petty, ugly remark he had ever made about her. He would not offer her false encouragement. He held no hope for her recovery and was certain she would meet her Maker soon. Even so, he would assure her comfort and make her feel loved and cared for. She would experience nothing but kindness and compassion in her last hours on earth.

He curled his hands around hers. "Please, Megan, forgive me for not being a better brother-in-law."

"Had we more time, we may have been friends." She sighed and turned away her face. Her breath crackled in her chest.

Michael tucked her hand along her side and pulled the covers up around her neck. He sat beside her and offered a prayer that she would find rest and relief from her pain.

Later that evening, after a quickly downed supper, Michael leaned against the rope barrier and gazed at the pink-and-orange-tinted clouds. As always, the brilliant display of God's handiwork filled him with awe.

Something was missing. Anne's singing. Before the sickness, each evening as the last rays of the sun shot over the distant mountains and before the noisy nocturnal cicadas and tree frogs dominated the night, Anne's soft soprano voice floated on the air as she sang lullabies to her nephews. The wagoners would still themselves and wait for the calming sound that brought back memories of home. Michael yearned to hear that peaceful sound again.

Anne joined him and stared down at her soiled clothing. "I must get myself clean."

She hurried behind the privacy screen, and then, with a bar of soap in her hand, she ducked under the rope and headed for the river.

"Wait, Anne," he called out. "You mustn't go alone."

He followed her to the bank of the river and leaned against a tree while she sat down and removed her shoes and stockings. She pulled off her mobcap and loosened her hair that flowed down to her waist.

Why, when they first met, had he assumed her hair was unremarkable brown? Streaks of muted gold shone and auburn tinted her tresses. How would it feel to run his fingers through those curls? The attraction shocked him. Desire had remained a stranger since the death of his wife.

The purple curtains of dusk closed over the sun as Anne waded into the waist-deep water, scrubbing the soap down her arms, over her clothes, and in her hair. She plunged down and disappeared under the water. When she resurfaced, she released the soap, turned her back to Michael, and buried her face in her hands. Her body shook, racked with her sobs.

Michael ran into the water, swept her up into his arms, and carried her up the bank. He sat on a blanket of moss at the base of a tree and cradled her in his arms until her crying subsided.

"I...I fear the boys may not survive." She pulled in a shaky breath and put her hand on Michael's chest. "They aren't taking any liquids. I tried everything. A spoon. A wet cloth. Wetting my fingers. Their tiny bodies can't endure long without water."

Michael curled his hand around hers and waited, prepared to listen, but she dropped her head against his shoulder. She lay still, and her breathing came softly and slowly. Was she sleeping? Their clothes were soaked, but he did not mind. He liked the feel of her curled against his body.

A movement in the rushes at the edge of the water caught his eye. A bird flittered among the reeds and hopped along the bank. Watching it tug a worm from the wet dirt, an idea struck him.

"Anne, Anne." He gently shook her. "I may have an answer."

"Wh-what?"

He gripped her shoulders and helped her stand. "What about this? You know how birds feed their babies by poking their beaks down their throats?"

Still a bit hazy, she furrowed her brow. "I think so."

"What if we place hollow reeds to the sides of the boys' throats and drizzle drops of water through them?"

"Maybe not water. That might make them strangle. But water thickened with sugar or honey." She cupped the side of Michael's face, and her eyes lit. "It might work."

He let her go, raced to a patch of reeds, and pulled a penknife from his waistcoat. He scooped up Anne's mobcap, shoes, and stockings and handed them to her. "You hurry and get out of those wet clothes. We can't have you getting sick. I'll cut lengths of reeds and be with you straight away."

"Oh, Michael, you've given me hope."

~

*M*ichael donned dry clothes and hurried to sit on the edge of the pallet next to Anne, William, and Gail, who cuddled both her boys close. David squirmed and moaned. Keith lay lethargic, unresponsive.

Anne settled David across her lap and waited for William to pull open his son's mouth. After dipping a reed in honey-laced water and filling its hollow insides, she pressed her finger on the tip of the reed and slid it into David's mouth along his cheek and to the side of his throat. He gagged, and she inched the reed out a bit. When he stopped resisting and seemed more comfortable, she removed her finger, allowing the liquid to flow down in tiny drips.

William frowned. "He's not swallowing."

"Maybe if you massage his throat," suggested Michael.

William circled his fingers around the base of David's neck. The little boy struggled a moment and then swallowed.

"Praise God," said Eleanor as she held a lantern overhead.

Hannah, who had stood beside Eleanor praying throughout the process, opened her eyes. "Praise Him, indeed." She motioned to Michael. "Should we try it on little Keith?"

Michael positioned the limp toddler in his lap, and once Hannah opened the boy's mouth, he tried several times to get him to swallow from a reed but without success.

Gail managed to lift herself up onto her elbow. "Please, little ones. Drink for mommy."

Her pitiful plea scraped Michael's heart and reminded him of a time when his daughter had been seriously ill with a chest inflammation. The coughing that wracked her tiny body, the feelings of helplessness, and the waiting had overwhelmed him. The fear of losing her had made him physically ill. Those memories caused sweat to break out on his brow.

As Anne continued to tend to David, she caught Michael's eye and lifted a brow. He shook his head.

She stretched her back. "Stop for now, Michael. I think David is tired too. Let them rest. We'll try again in a while."

Hannah stood and brushed the wrinkles from her petticoats. "The Bankses are calling for me. I'll be back when I can."

At that moment, Mr. Johnson, accompanied by Grady and Joan Daniels and Preston Hudson, approached the rope barrier.

Michael sprung up and held out his hand. "Don't come any closer, please."

"We'll stay safe, Michael," said Mr. Johnson, cradling a small harp in his arms. "But we'd like to have a watch-night service. Something we Methodists do...a gathering to encourage us to pray and reflect and lift up one another."

Mr. Daniels stepped forward. "We'd like to share our worship. Lord knows, we need Him more than ever now. We'd like to sing a hymn John Wesley wrote especially for watch-night."

Anne, Eleanor, William, and Molly left their patients and gathered together with Michael as the wagoners sang. Michael was not familiar with the lyrics, but some of the words caught his attention and tugged at his heart.

> *Jesus, God of our salvation,*
> *Give us eyes thyself to see,*
> *Waiting for thy consolation,*
> *Longing to believe on thee:*
> *Now vouchsafe the sacred power,*
> *Now the faith divine impart;*
> *Meet us at this solemn hour,*

Shine in every drooping heart.

Michael locked gazes with Anne, whose eyes glistened with unshed tears.

Dear Lord, our hearts are drooping. I beseech You, bolster Anne as she cares for Your sheep. Grant me Your grace to know what to do and say that will honor You.

When the watch-night grew to a close, Michael's heart felt lighter, and the ache in his chest abated. He returned to the Forbeses' pallet and, renewed in spirit, tried again to help Keith to take nourishment from the reed, but to no avail.

Deep into the night, he fell asleep at the foot of the covers only inches away from Anne. He woke briefly to find the moon shining on her face. Succumbed to exhaustion, she slept heavily with her arms wrapped tightly around her. He sat up and draped a cover over her, then fell back to sleep. He had not dozed long when a tap on his shoulder brought him awake.

"Michael," Hannah whispered. "It's Megan." She hesitated. "She has passed."

Trying not to awaken Anne and the Forbeses, he arose and crept over to where Megan lay a couple of yards away. He bent down and listened for her breath. She was indeed gone.

Dear Lord, she is with You now.

Amelia, lying on the bedding next to her friend, turned onto her side and stared at him. "Oh, please, not Megan." She pressed her face into her covers to muffle her cries.

"Michael?" Anne rolled onto her stomach and watched him.

He shook his head.

She sat up onto her knees. "I'm so sorry."

She reached over William as he began to stir and felt David's forehead. The relief on her face told Michael that the boy had improved. She touched Keith, and her face crumpled.

"He left us about an hour ago," said Gail, cradling her son's lifeless body. "I wanted a little more time before I had to let him go."

Anne started to cry, and the pain in Michael's chest hurt as if he had cracked a rib.

Two precious souls had departed in the night and now dwelled with the angels in heaven.

CHAPTER 7

The following afternoon, Anne did not attend the burial but remained with David. His color had improved despite the lesions that covered his torso, and he drank honey-flavored tea without the need for a reed and without coaxing.

Gail had sobbed for hours until she vomited. Despite her over-wrought state, she insisted on attending the service that the wagon master officiated. William carried her to the gravesite, remaining at a distance from the others. A half hour after the others left for the service, David fell asleep, and Anne took the opportunity to speak with Amelia. The woman had adored her childhood friend. Grief and illness made it difficult for her to take deep breaths. Her fever was gone but had left her spent, barely able to sit up.

Anne sat beside Amelia on her bedding and pressed calamine paste onto the pustules that covered her arms and legs. She took extra care with the ones on her forehead, the only part of her face exposed by the scarf she had covered herself with. Some lesions were deep and would leave scars.

Not something Anne would mention, as the woman obviously took great pride in her beauty. Anne touched the two blemishes on her own temple, and her heart ached for Amelia. Her scars would be much worse.

"This should bring relief soon. I'll leave the jar for you to finish." Anne corked the jar of calamine and folded the cloth she would add to a pile to be boiled later.

"The paste feels nice and cool, but the itching is unbearable." Amelia lifted her fingers to her face.

Anne tugged her hand. "Try not to scratch. And, please, leave the gloves on."

Amelia gazed at the wagons. "What am I to do? I came here with my dearest friend. When she came home to Scotland to help attend to our aunt's estate, we devised a plan. I would return to the colonies with her and find a husband in Graniteville. We would be next-door neighbors. Bring up our children and grow old together." She sighed. "My...how my fortunes have changed."

Anne stretched out her tired legs and covered them with her petticoats. "Is going back home an option?"

"Not really. I have no family left to speak of." Amelia lay back on her elbows. "I've had my eye on Michael. He has means. Status. And he's quite handsome. He'd make a good catch, would he not?"

A good catch? Was that how she thought of Michael?

Anne bridled her temper. "Michael is a fine man. Any woman would be fortunate to have his love."

Amelia scoffed. "Love? It isn't my main concern, though it might come later. But it will take all my wiles to win him over. He will resist me. Megan informed me that he has never recovered from his wife's death. I shall befriend his daughter and I must work even harder to charm him into ignoring my scars. I may enjoy the challenge."

How did Amelia propose to face such a challenge when it

was obvious she and Michael could not properly travel together now that his sister-in-law had passed?

Anne had had quite enough conversation with Amelia and stood. "Excuse me. I must see to the others."

At that moment, something caught her eye at the back of the boundary. Three Indian men leaned against the rope. One scanned her from head to toe. She clasped her throat but could not make a sound.

They started to duck under the rope when one of them jabbed the other with his elbow and pointed to Charlotte and Elspeth and then to the other patients napping on their pallets. Panic filled their eyes, and they mumbled among themselves before backing away quickly and disappearing into the woods.

Michael entered the shelter area followed by the other mourners. William carried Gail to their pallet where their son slept soundly and then joined Anne.

Michael stared at Anne's face. "What is amiss?"

"Indians. Three of them. I nearly fainted."

Michael scanned the woods. "Did they approach?"

"I believe they intended to but changed their minds when they saw our patients. The terror in their eyes was quite something. They couldn't depart fast enough."

Mr. Cooper, standing nearby, gripped the rope barrier. "Can you describe them?"

"Not well. They were here only a few seconds."

"Their clothing?" Mr. Cooper coaxed.

Anne wrinkled her brow. "They didn't wear shirts. One of them wore two necklaces. One made of shells and the other a rawhide string with a crescent moon ornament."

"What about their hair? And did you see a black snake tattoo or decoration anywhere?" The wagon master's expression grew taut.

"Their heads were shaved." Anne touched her mobcap.

"Except for topknots with feathers in them. And no black snake decorations that I recall."

"Sounds like Cherokee. They're not usually hostile. They were more than likely curious. They must've got quite a scare seeing the pox, which means they'll steer clear of us." He scrutinized the sick. "That's the only good thing that's come from this hellish business."

Mr. Cooper searched Anne's eyes. "You've done well, but you look exhausted. I know it comes not only from the work, but from the loss of your nephew. I couldn't be sorrier."

Anne gulped and clasped her arms across her waist as shards of pain slashed through her body. Michael stepped close, his shoulder inches from hers, close enough to feel his warmth. The small gesture comforted her.

"I don't mean to press you, Anne." Mr. Cooper rested his arm on the pistol tucked into his belt. "But no one's come down with the pox in days. How much longer, do you think, before we can get back on the trail?"

Anne glanced over her shoulder at the Smythe girls. "We need to wait until the sores clear. About five or six more days, I would guess."

Would more wagoners succumb to the pox? The rigors of caring for the sick had seriously depleted her stamina.

Lord, I beseech You for strength.

~

*F*our days later, Anne and Hannah boiled the clothes and coverings touched by the sick. The midafternoon air stifled as much as the steam rising from the cast-iron vat. Anne wiped her face and neck with a handkerchief, then shoved it into her apron pocket.

The recovering patients either stood together or sat on the

bench Michael had fashioned out of eight-foot wooden railings resting on tree stumps.

"It's called a deacon's seat," Michael had explained when setting it up. "We use them in bunkhouses to give the loggers places to sit or play games."

What would she have done without Michael? During the entire ordeal, he had been ever-present, ready and willing to assist in any way. His encouraging words had bolstered her often when sadness threatened. Today, he waited nearby with a long stick, ready to remove the boiling-hot pieces of laundry and throw them across the rope barrier to dry.

Gratitude was not all she felt. She had become intensely aware of him. Her heart fluttered when he neared and ached when he left.

Hannah stirred the bubbling water with a wooden paddle. "Thank goodness I had this pot I make my candles in."

"Indeed," Anne replied offhandedly.

William and Gail huddled at the far end of the shelter speaking in furtive whispers. Defiant, Gail crossed her arms across her chest. Furious, William locked his arms stiffly by his sides. He thrust his hands in the air, ducked under the rope, and stomped toward the woods.

Anne wiped her hands on her apron and started to follow him.

"You're leaving?" Michael asked.

"William seems upset. He may need me."

Michael dropped the stick he had been holding. "Should I accompany you?"

"No, thank you." Anne smiled. "I appreciate your concern."

She hurried past her distraught sister-in-law, who had covered her face with her hands. Her shoulders shook with her sobs, but Anne knew from experience that in her present state, Gail might rebuff any attempts to comfort her.

Anne reached William as he halted beside his son's grave. Grass had started to sprout in the dark soil. Nature was already reclaiming the site. She could hardly bear to look at it.

She touched her brother's shoulder. "What is amiss, William?"

Anger distorted his face, and anxiety filled his usually lively eyes. He jammed his arms by his sides.

What could be so dire?

"Gail. It's Gail. She refuses to go on. She wants to go back home...to Scotland."

"What!" This *was* dire news.

"She is beside herself with grief. She says she's lost one child to this place and refuses to surrender another." William paced, his hands balled into fists. "She wants her mother."

"Would she change her mind...given time?"

"We don't have time. You know Mr. Cooper told everyone last night that our wagon train will be back on the road in two days. Two days!" He yanked off his hat and raked his fingers through his hair. "I fear for Gail's health and her mental state if I force her to go on." He held out his hands to her, entreating. "What are we to do, Anne?"

"Let me talk to her." She hugged him. "We'll find an answer."

Anne left him and trudged back to the shelter to face Gail, whose tear-stained cheeks were bloody red. Tendrils of her hair had escaped her mobcap and hung loose. Her overly bright eyes worried Anne most.

"William told me. Let's sit at the table and talk."

Gail shook her head violently and pressed claw-like fingers against her breast. "Don't bother. There's nothing you can say that will change my mind."

"I know you grieve, dearest, but making such a crucial decision when you are in this state might not be for the best. Why don't you continue on with the train and give it more thought? Then, in a few days, you may change your mind."

Gail trembled. "No. I want to go home. I hate this country."

"What of William's plans for a new life in Camden? He has such hopes."

"What of *my* loss? *My* feelings? Do they count for nothing?"

"Of course, they count. But you have come this far—"

"Stop. Please stop pressuring me, Anne. I cannot bear it." She broke down in sobs so fierce it started David crying.

"Auntie Anne, what's wrong with mama?" David called out from the pallet.

He kept wailing until Hannah picked him up and walked with him around the shelter area, rubbing his back and cooing.

William returned and hugged his wife. "Hush, my dear. We will do as you wish. We will return home. I'm sure my employer will give me my job back."

What of William's desire to partner in his own printing shop? He must be crushed. He had not only lost a child—he had lost his dream.

What of her own dreams?

The questions bombarding Anne's mind overwhelmed her, and she fled. She had retreated yards into the forest when she heard footsteps behind her. She whirled around.

Michael halted several feet away, a hand resting on the pistol secured in his belt. "It's not safe for you to be alone out here, Anne."

She bent over and pressed her hands to her roiling stomach. "I am undone."

"My friend, I'm here and I'm prepared to listen to whatever you may want to share." His expressive eyes held concern.

Michael thought of her as his friend.

"I don't think my family will be travelling on to Camden. Grief has so overtaken my sister-in-law, William fears for her sanity. She refuses to continue on with the wagon train and insists on returning home to Scotland."

A muscle in Michael's jaw twitched. "That is sad news, indeed."

"Sad in many more ways than you can imagine."

He raised an eyebrow.

"I don't want to go back. All that awaits me there are constant reminders of my precious Keith." She choked. "I loved him as my own, you know." Her eyes blurred with unshed tears. "I dunno think I can bear it."

Michael shifted from one foot to the other. "So it's the memories you would encounter of your nephew that keep you from going back?"

Anne nodded. "Partly. As much as I adore my family, I have lived their life far too long. I don't want to return to the way things were before." She glanced toward the circled wagons. "It's difficult to explain, but there's something about this country. Being around the people on this train. Hearing about their hopes and dreams has inspired me in a way I haven't been in years. I crave more than what I had. I dream of becoming an independent woman...a tailor...with my own shop."

"That's a fine dream, Anne." He took a step closer. "And one I might be able to help you fulfill."

~

"Come. Let's sit over there." Michael took Anne by her elbow and led her to sit beside him on a fallen tree trunk. "I have been contemplating my own dilemma, and you may be my answer."

Anne cocked her head.

"Amelia insists that despite Megan's death, she wants to continue on to Graniteville. Apparently, she has no family to return to. Her decision has left me in an awkward position. In all propriety, she and I, both unmarried, cannot continue to travel together."

"I imagine not."

He hesitated a moment before angling his knees toward hers, searching for words to phrase his proposal so as not to insult Anne's age. "Would you be amenable to travel with us as her companion? That way, you could be chaperones each for the other."

Her eyebrows shot up.

"Graniteville is a thriving town and would be an ideal place for you to open a tailor shop." He leaned forward. "I would pay you, of course."

He studied her stoic face but could not guess her reaction.

Her eyes clouded. "I have wondered why you escorted Megan and Amelia and not your brother."

She had changed the subject. To avoid his proposal?

"Originally, my brother...Cal...was to meet them in Philadelphia. But he had an accident, broke his leg two weeks before he was to leave."

She stretched out her legs and crossed her ankles, then folded her hands and dropped them onto her lap. "I'm sorry to hear that."

The past couple of weeks had taken some of the starch out of her, and Michael longed to put his arm around her drooping shoulders. For the first time, he noticed a spattering of freckles across her nose and cheeks.

Heather's creamy complexion had been perfection. Was calling Anne *friend* a way of erecting a barrier between them? He mentally shook himself. *Return to the subject at hand.*

"What do you think of my offer?"

She looked him squarely in the eye, and once again, he saw the golden flecks among the brown. "I believe it's something I would very much desire to do."

Michael's heart lurched. His strong reaction surprised him.

"But I must have my brother's blessing."

He swallowed hard. "Of course."

She stood and faced him. "May I give you my answer tomorrow?"

Michael nodded, but waiting for Anne's reply proved surprisingly hard and made for a very long night.

CHAPTER 8

"You would leave our family? Leave me?" William was incredulous. "And go to a strange place... alone? I cannot fathom it."

Gail patted his back. "Calm yourself, my dear. Anne has a right to choose the life she wants."

They had left the shelter to return to their wagon for the first time since the pox had struck the wagoners. Anne had waited until after supper to broach the subject, while they sat on kegs away from the fire. David, weary and sleepy-eyed, sat on his mother's lap.

The reactions from Gail and William proved to be the exact opposite of what she had anticipated. She had imagined Gail would protest and William would understand.

"I won't be completely alone. Michael and Amelia will accompany me to Graniteville."

"You hardly know them." William put his balled fists on his knees.

"You've come to know Michael over the past weeks. He is as fine a gentleman as I've ever known."

William shrugged. "Yes. I will grant you that. But what do you know about running a shop? Managing a business?"

Anne gave him a mischievous smile. "You remember Mr. Gordon, the owner of the tailor shop in our village? Well, for the past two years, I have visited him often, gleaning all the knowledge I could."

William raised an eyebrow. "So you've been planning this for years and kept it a secret from me?"

Anne shrugged. "Dear brother, until we decided to come to the colonies, I didn't mention it because I wasn't sure it would ever come to pass. There wasn't enough business in our village for two tailor shops."

"Humph." He shook his head. "And what about funds?"

"For years, I've been saving the money I've made from all the tailoring and seamstressing I've done."

"Again, you had plans in mind without consulting with me. Am I such an ogre that you felt the need for secrecy? All this time, I believed you were content with your life."

The hurt on his face saddened Anne. "You are the furthest thing from an ogre in this world. The last thing I want to do is cause you pain. Please believe me." She glanced at the circled wagons. "Something has happened to me here in the colonies. The yearning of the people I encounter to make something of themselves. To be free...to make their own decisions. It's awakened my spirit."

For the first time since they started the conversation, a hint of admiration shone in her brother's eyes. Of course, he understood her longings. He had dreamed of a new life of his own. A dream he had chosen to relinquish to assuage his wife's grief.

"Can we not help Anne in some way?" Gail kissed the top of David's head. "Is she not due her part of the inheritance?"

Anne's spirits leapt. She had truly forgotten about the bequest from their parents. Her sister-in-law's support made Anne love her even more.

William stared down at his hands resting in his lap.

What was he thinking? How would he respond? Anne's pulse hammered.

"It is quite a sum, Anne. Too much for you to care for on a journey such as this. I'll ask Michael to keep it safe and to manage it for you."

Though she desired independence, a man's oversight was obligatory. Besides her brother, no one held her trust more than Michael, despite the short time they had been acquainted. William's proposal made sense. Then, at once, his true meaning dawned on her.

"Does that...I have your permission?"

William stood and held out his arms. "How can I deny you your dream, dear sister?"

Anne ran into his embrace and wrapped her arms around his waist. His body was solid...comforting...home.

He would no longer be there for her. What was she doing?

"I shall miss you, Anne." He cleared his throat and peered at David. "I cannot imagine our lives without you."

Holding David in her arms, Gail joined in their hug. "I mentioned once before how much we have relied on you, Anne. I shall miss you terribly, but it's time for me to take on more responsibility for my family. And I dearly desire a life of happiness for you."

Gail's face, now free of scabs, was pale except for the dark circles underneath eyes which exposed a deep sorrow.

A twinge of regret twisted in Anne's chest. Should she leave them in their mutual time of grief? Was she being selfish? No, it was her moment. She had prayed fervently, and God had made a path for her.

David held out his arms to her. "You are going away, Auntie Anne?"

Her nephew had remained silent throughout the conversation, but apparently, even at the tender age of four, he understood. He grieved, too, often asking after his little brother. One of the most difficult times in her life had occurred as she and Gail listened to William trying to explain Keith's death to him. Losing his auntie would add to his unhappiness. Guilt reared its ugly head, casting doubt on her decisions. She opened her arms, cuddled him on her lap, and kissed the top of his head. Overwhelmed by the thought of leaving him, she embraced him too tightly.

"You're squishing me, Auntie." He patted her cheek.

Laughing through her tears, Anne bounced him on her knees. "So sorry, little one. I'm squishing because I love you so very much."

Gail held out her arms for her son. "It's time for a nap. I may take one myself."

Once Gail settled underneath the wagon, Anne searched for the words she wanted to share with her brother.

Hoping she would not cry, she began. "William, you must know how torn I am by this decision. I yearn to fulfill my dreams, but my heart breaks to think I may never see you again." She glanced at Gail. "Do you think it at all possible that once you reach Philadelphia and civilization, Gail will have calmed down enough for you to reason with her?"

William shook his head. "I don't know. It's possible, but I've never seen her as she is. Frankly, it's frightening."

"Coping with Gail's suffering as well as your own grief—"

"I'll be fine. Don't worry about me."

Though Anne knew worrying would not add a single hour to her life, she suffered it often.

"Michael says Graniteville is a thriving settlement. They may need a printer. Maybe...if you stay in the city for a while, and Gail has had some time, you could broach the subject of joining me there. If that's something you would want?"

A flicker of hope shone in his eyes. "I'll give it thought and prayer."

She hugged him. "I'm quite overwhelmed with so many emotions, dear brother. I truly feel that Michael's offer is a godsend."

William stepped back and cleared his throat. "I shall have a long talk with him. I must satisfy some particulars before I place you in his care."

What would it mean—being placed in Michael's care? He would be her employer and a friend safeguarding her finances.

Did she desire for him to be more? If so, would she be willing to fight for him against Amelia with her many advantages—beauty, money, experience?

CHAPTER 9

*A*n early-morning mist hung in the air, tingling the hairs on Anne's arms as she stood next to Michael while waiting for the others to hitch their horses.

Transferring her trunks, one with personal belongings and one with tailoring supplies, had taken only a few minutes. The hugs and kisses for her family took longer. Letting go of David, his bottom lip trembling, hurt so much that doubts crept in once more.

William guided his wagon out of the clearing and maneuvered it to turn north back to Philadelphia. At the tail end of the circled train, the Smythes and the Tanners waved goodbye to him, and when William waved back, a strange hollow feeling permeated Anne's body. Her family...the people she loved most in the world...were leaving.

Would she ever see them again? What was she doing? Part of her panicked and ached to run after them.

"Second thoughts?" Michael waved back to David, who was bouncing up and down on Gail's lap.

"And third...and fourth." She folded her arms across her midriff.

"You'll be fine, Anne. You are with me...and Amelia now. You'll be starting a new life full of promise. You'll love Graniteville. It's quite beautiful, and some of the nicest people I've ever known live there."

His face, eyes, and entire countenance softened. He loved his home. Did he realize how his words encouraged her and lifted her spirits? He was a kind man. How she longed to reach over and twine her fingers through his.

Mr. Cooper rode past, tipping his hat first to Amelia on the wagon seat, and then to Anne. "Morning. I'll give the call for us to start in a few minutes."

"Mr. Cooper, will my brother be safe? They'll be a single wagon without others to protect them."

The wagon master nodded. "I believe he'll be safe. As you experienced, there are many settlements and farms between here and Philadelphia. Our passage through that region went smoothly and with no rivers to cross. Unlike up ahead." He scanned the wagons. "I must go. See if the others are prepared." He headed off to the spread the message.

Michael climbed onto the wagon seat next to Amelia and clasped the reins. "You're fine with walking, Anne?"

"I prefer it, thank you." It would give her solitude, time to mull over her choices. And she would not have to listen to Amelia's vapid attempts to capture Michael's attention.

"Wagons! Ho!" Mr. Cooper's gravelly shout echoed through the woods.

Anne was so deep in thought, she jerked as if someone had poked her with a stick.

Their wagon was third in line for the day. When it came their turn to move onto the trail, she looked behind her for her family, but they had already traveled out of sight...north...and possibly out of her life forever. She headed south. Her entire body quivered with anticipation.

Lord, what do You have in store for me?

～

*T*he following week as they traversed through the foothills of the Virginia mountains, the wagoners fell into a routine. Michael appreciated the orderliness—rising before dawn, then eating a hearty breakfast of johnnycakes, bacon, eggs, or porridge. Weather and trail conditions permitting, they covered around five to eight miles before noon when they stopped for a cold lunch, usually ham or bacon, bread, and cheese. After luncheon, they would travel another ten miles or so before making camp around seven in a place scouted out by Mr. Sanders, often in a meadow or a break in the forest used by previous wagon trains.

Fording streams slowed their pace. On one occasion, Mr. Sanders offered to take Anne across a shallow stream on his horse. Michael observed them closely as the scout held her by her waist and placed her on the saddle. He said something that made her laugh. He mounted in front of her, wrapped her arms around his waist, and put one of his arms over hers. When they reached the far side of the stream, the scout held onto Anne a bit longer than necessary after helping her dismount. From then on, when they crossed rivers and streams, Michael coaxed Anne to join him and Amelia on the wagon seat.

Rainy days that turned the trail to muck found Anne huddling inside the wagon with Amelia. On temperate days, she chatted with other wagoners stationed in front or behind. He missed her then, especially when she walked out of his sight.

Michael enjoyed the evenings the most, when after supper people gathered in small, intimate groups to share stories, sing hymns, or sit in quiet companionship.

Each night, Anne would sit near a lantern, her head bowed, shoulders hunched, laboring over the sewing tasks the others brought her.

A shrewd but fair businesswoman, she amazed him with her bartering. In exchange for a wool vest, Mr. Johnson made her a pair of latchet shoes. Eleanor Tanner requested a cravat to give her husband for his birthday. She traded a supply of goat's milk and cheese for the rest of their journey. Mrs. Banks and Amelia, who had both lost weight from having smallpox, needed dresses altered. Mrs. Banks offered a couple of her beautifully fashioned delicate lace collars. Amelia paid her two pence, pie-shaped pieces cut from a Spanish coin, which Anne informed Michael she stored in a tin box inside her trunk of personal belongings.

Michael had a discerning eye for fashion. He had frequented some of the most sought-after tailors in the colonies. Anne's impeccable clothing rivaled their work. She would thrive in Graniteville.

Sometimes he would catch her gazing out toward the forest with a somber expression, her shoulders slumped. Did she grieve Keith's death, or was she missing her family? Was she questioning her decision to go with him?

Was he fooling himself that his feelings for her were only of friendship? They changed with every conversation, every smile, and the touch of her hands on his shoulders when she allowed him to help her down from the wagon. Not since his wife died had he desired a deeper relationship with a woman, one based on trust where they both felt safe and encouraged to share confidences. More and more, he longed to embrace Anne, to let her know she was not alone.

One evening after supper, Michael returned from visiting the Daniels brothers and came upon Anne and Amelia seated on barrels near a waning campfire.

"Anne?" Amelia tucked her legs under her dress. "You are from Scotland, but you don't have an accent. Just a word or two here and there."

Michael, pausing at the back of the wagon, had wondered that himself and anticipated her response.

Anne continued sewing. "I grew up in England. We moved to Scotland when I was thirteen."

"Ah." Amelia nodded. "If you don't mind my asking, why did you never marry?"

Michael stretched forward, eager to hear Anne's response.

Anne stopped sewing and wove the needle into the cloth. "I don't mind. I was engaged once...when I was nineteen." She stared into the fire. "His name was James. He belonged to a group of Scots, the Black Watch. They were formed to keep the Highlands safe from crime."

Michael had heard of the Black Watch and was familiar with their sad story.

"The regiment was called to London on the pretense of being inspected by King George. But when they arrived, they discovered that the king wasn't there. They first heard rumors that they would be sent to the war in Austria. That was another lie. They were being sent to the West Indies. All they wanted was to go home to Scotland. Feeling betrayed, they mutinied."

"Oh, my," Amelia exclaimed.

"Their leaders were imprisoned in the Tower of London, where they were shot by a firing squad. The rest, including my Jamie, were sent to Jamaica." Anne touched her fingers to her throat. "He died of a fever not long after he arrived. It broke my heart. The sadness has never left me."

Though Michael felt a bit guilty eavesdropping, the information he gleaned explained much about Anne. The loss of her beloved fiancé had caused her to substitute her brother's family for one she might have had. Her choice to leave that safe situation to become an independent woman doubled his admiration for her.

Amelia sighed. "I am sorry, Anne."

Michael stepped from behind the wagon and joined them.

Anne rolled her shoulders and stretched her neck back and forth. She straightened her spine and winced.

"You work too hard." Michael sat on a barrel beside her. "And I've noticed you bending lower to see your work. Maybe you should limit yourself. The lantern light isn't good for your eyes."

"I appreciate your concern, but I'm accustomed to it."

As Amelia looked back and forth at them, a frown wrinkled her brow, and she cleared her throat. "I understand we will be visiting a settlement tomorrow. You will escort us, of course?"

Michael grinned. "Of course. I look forward to showing off my lovely ladies."

Amelia patted the curls she had cut to frame her face and hide the deep pock marks along her hairline. Though the blemishes must sting her pride, to Amelia's credit, she had not allowed the hurt to show.

Anne folded the vest and put it into her sewing box. "Time for me to retire." She yawned and stretched her arms over her head.

Did she realize how sensual her movements were?

"I'll bid you goodnight as well," said Amelia.

He watched Amelia fold herself into the hammock strung between the wagon and a post. Since the wagon was too hot for sleeping, she had claimed the hammock for her own. Anne slept on the ground beneath a canvas tied to the wagon bed and poles. He made sure they were both secure before checking the dying embers and rolling underneath the wagon and onto his pallet.

He drifted into a peaceful sleep, but not before deciding on a way to help Anne at the settlement.

Would she go along with him?

∾

*E*arly evening the following day, Anne's spirits were heightened as she strolled arm-in-arm with Michael and Amelia along the main street of the Wilkes Gorge settlement, a town with thirty mostly Scots-Irish family residences, a mercantile, trading post and tavern, blacksmith, carpenter shop, and Presbyterian church.

Anne glanced right and left. "I'm surprised. I hadn't expected such a large settlement."

"A fine place to celebrate a special day." Michael stopped walking.

Amelia raised an eyebrow. "What is your meaning, Michael?"

"It's July first. Anne's birthday." Mischief lit his eyes.

"My birthday?" Anne tapped fingers to her heart. "I hadn't realized. I lost track of time and wasn't even aware of today's date. How did you know?"

"William told me. We are to 'make merry,' he said."

It was so like her William, trying to ensure her happiness even though they were apart. A twinge of homesickness tugged at her, but she fought it. Her brother desired it to be a happy day.

Amelia clapped her hands. "Felicitations, Anne. How shall we proceed?"

Anne glanced at the sign overhead. "This carpenter shop. I should very much like to explore it."

Amelia scoffed. "Whatever for?"

Michael rolled his eyes at her.

Managing to look sheepish, Amelia said, "After all, it is your birthday...your choice."

The bell over the door tingled as they entered, and Anne breathed in the pleasant aroma of cedar mingled with the smell of newly cut wood.

A man wearing a leather apron pinned to the front of his

shirt wiped his hands on a cloth and greeted them. "Good day. May I be of assistance?"

Michael bowed. "My friend here was curious about your work. May we look about?"

The proprietor returned Michael's bow. "You may."

Anne walked to a row of rocking chairs, sat in one, and preceded to rock. She ran her fingers over the dark vines thickly woven together to form the arms. "What is it made of?"

"It's one of my wife's creations. She fashions them out of willow branches."

Anne leaned her head back, closed her eyes, and pressed her toes against the floor. "This is ever so comfortable." She opened her eyes and caught Michael staring at her. She reluctantly stood up but pushed against the chair arm to make it rock. "Please tell your wife how much I enjoyed the chair. She has a gift."

The man dipped his head. "She'll be mighty pleased to hear it."

They stepped outside, and Anne caught the attention of Eleanor and Oliver Tanner as they entered the blacksmith's farther down the street. They smiled and returned her wave.

"Where to next?" Amelia asked.

"Let's go to the mercantile. I have something in mind." Michael folded their arms through his again and led them down the street.

Inside the store, Anne made a beeline for the rolls of materials and the notions. "I can't believe the variety of buttons."

Amelia scoffed and rummaged through a pile of ribbons. "Only you would be excited about buttons."

Michael left them to talk to the proprietor, but they spoke in such low tones, Anne could not make out what they said. The man left for the back room and came back with several leather pouches.

Michael motioned to Anne. "Come. I have something for you."

Anne joined him at the counter, and Amelia hovered close behind.

Michael opened one of the pouches and held up a pair of wire-rimmed spectacles. "Try these."

Anne tucked in her chin. "What?"

His expression was so eager, she could not refuse him. She placed the lenses across the bridge of her nose and curved the side pieces around her ears.

She blinked a few times and scanned the room. "Things are a bit blurry."

"Here." The store owner handed her another pair. "You may not need such a strong correction."

Anne tried on the second pair, picked up a leaflet lying on the counter, and started reading the fine print. "I'm amazed. It's so clear."

"Ha! I knew you were struggling with your sewing." Michael put his fingertip under her chin and tilted her face up to his. "Happy birthday, Anne."

Tears pooled in Anne's eyes. How could she ever thank him for this wonderful gift?

Amelia giggled. "They make your eyes huge. You look like a schoolmarm."

She *was* twenty-nine today. Well and truly a spinster. But now a spinster who could see. That Michael noticed her poor eyesight and sought out a solution moved her. Without thinking, she clasped him around his waist and pressed her cheek into his chest.

"It's a delightful gift, Michael." His heart thundered against her face. His body was warm...solid.

Amelia cleared her throat, and Anne stepped back.

Michael addressed the proprietor. "We'll take two pairs as a precaution."

"Thank you again, Michael."

He paid for the eyeglasses and waited for the man to wrap them in brown paper and tie them with a string. "May I keep them for you until we return to the wagon train?"

"If you would."

He tucked the package into the inside pocket of his waistcoat near the place where Anne had rested her head against him.

Had she actually abandoned propriety and hugged him? Heat rose in her cheeks.

"Now, if you would help me with something." Michael motioned to a table laden with rolls of fabric.

She joined him. "Yes?"

"I want to purchase some cloth...to make a dress...for my daughter, Caitlin. Or Cate, as I call her."

Ah, yes. He spoke of the daughter Megan had mentioned when Anne had overheard her and Amelia's plan to win him over.

Anne touched one of the bolts of material. "Tell me what she's like and what the dress will be for."

"She's nine and slender." Michael tapped just below his chest. "And comes to here on me. She has moss-green eyes like her mother and black hair like me."

His obvious love for his daughter shone in his eyes and made Anne's insides go soft.

"She likes climbing trees and most often wears breeches and shirts. So she needs encouragement to wear dresses. This one would be for Sunday services." He cocked his head. "Would you make it for her?"

The appeal in the depths of his voice was irresistible.

"It would be my pleasure."

Anne shuffled through the fabrics until she found a length of green cotton with the tiniest of pink flowers in the pattern and held it up for Michael to consider. "I think this will suit. It's lovely, but cotton is quite expensive. What say you?"

"I trust your judgement. And cost is not an issue." His smile was infectious.

"Should I add a hat, gloves, stockings, and ribbon?"

"Yes, let's do this well. Anything for my Cate."

What a fine man and caring father. For a moment, she recalled her own dear father. Those remembrances brought thoughts of William. She missed them both.

"You will manage this, then?" Michael asked.

"I will." Anne picked up the material, her mind already alive with choosing the embellishments and accessories.

Michael walked toward the door. "You ladies keep shopping. I have something I must attend to. Take your time. I'll return soon."

Amelia selected a straw hat and two lengths of blue ribbon. "Here, Anne," she said, placing the hat on top of Anne's mobcap and tying the ribbons over the top of the hat and into a bow at the back of her neck. "My gift for you. And these ribbons should brighten you up a bit, in contrast to the brown you so often wear."

"How kind of you." Anne pressed the folds in her dress that, as Amelia had pointed out, was a dull brown.

Spurred by that observation, she purchased material with tiny yellow flowers on a background of blue, the same hue as the ribbons. It suited. New life...new colors. She would begin sewing it as soon as she completed her other projects.

Michael rejoined them as she finished selecting hanks of thread and paying for her purchases using the earnings he had given her the day before. An amount too generous by far.

After paying for the materials for Cate, Michael tucked their packages underneath his arms and escorted them outside. "I'm famished, ladies. What say we have dinner at the tavern?"

"Oh, let's." Amelia clasped his forearm. "I'm so very tired of the wagon train fare."

They walked the short distance to the tavern, and when they entered, the Tanners, Ezra and Claire Banks, and Mr. Johnson waved her over to their table.

Eleanor jumped up from her chair and gave Anne a bear hug. "Happy birthday, Anne!"

Anne sat down, and Michael sat next to her, his eyes dancing with delight.

She leaned over and whispered to him, "You arranged this?"

"I did. I tried to find the others, but they had already left for the campsite." He cocked his head. "You are pleased?"

"I don't think I have ever had a happier birthday. Thank you." She put her hand on the table. "Though, I do miss my family."

He covered her hand with his. "I hope you will consider us your family now."

From friend to family. Looking down at his hand, Anne wanted more. She wanted his love. Wanted him to feel the same way she felt about him. There it was—she loved him. She had resisted the emotion. In fear of rejection? The acknowledgement stunned and nearly took her breath away.

Michael squeezed her fingers. "Are you all right?"

Before she could answer, the waitress arrived with their dinner.

Overcome by her revelation, could Anne swallow anything?

Once the others tucked into their shepherd's pie, she forced herself to join in. It tasted delicious, and she found herself enjoying the fare, especially the warm, freshly baked bread slathered with creamy butter.

The waitress placed lighted lanterns across the counter and lit candles positioned around the room. The candles atop the fireplace mantel were secured in mounds of wax that dripped over the edge in long strings. The flickering light cast soft shadows across the faces of her new and dear friends.

The remaining patrons finished their meals and left, leaving behind an atmosphere of an intimate family gathering.

By the end of the meal, Anne felt more relaxed than she had been in quite some time. Was it the tankard of ale, the laughter, the pleasant company, or the warmth of Michael's body when he leaned close?

Mr. Johnson adjusted the eyeglasses he had pushed up onto his forehead. "What a fine meal. But now it is time for gifts."

Anne sat up, her eyes wide. "You shouldn't have—"

"Hush now," Claire said. "Our gifts not only celebrate your birthday, but are our way of thanking you for all you did for us. You cared for me and brought me through the pox. My Ezra and I will always be in your debt."

Anne looked down at the table. "I only did what I could."

"I'll be first." Mr. Johnson slid a small package to Michael, who passed it along to Anne.

Delighted, Anne opened the package that held a pair of shoe strings.

"It's not much," said Mr. Johnson. "They'll be useful for when you wear your latchet shoes."

"It's a fine gift, Mr. Johnson."

He leaned forward. "Would you gift me with the use of my given name? It's Simon. I was named after a Simon in the Bible who was also a shoemaker."

Anne smiled at him. "I'd be honored, Simon, if you call me Anne."

Ezra pulled a package from inside his waistcoat and handed it to his wife, who gave it to Anne. "I hope you like it."

Anne untied the string and opened the paper to find a thatch of thread that she held up to the candlelight. "It's the finest I've ever seen."

"I make it by hatchelling flax. Combing it through paddles with nails, over and over until the thread is like corn silk. Many women use it for embroidery," Claire explained. "Your work is so fine, I'm hoping you will find use for it."

"I'll treasure it, Claire."

Eleanor, seated next to Anne, pushed a package toward her. "Our gift is a practical one, but one we think you will make good use of."

Curious, Anne tore into the paper to expose a three-inch by eight-inch piece of stone.

"It's a whetstone for sharpening your shears," said Oliver. "The blacksmith assured us that since it's made of quartz, it will last a long time."

"What a brilliant gift. I shall think of you every time I use it." Tears welled in Anne's eyes. "I thank you, all of you, for your gifts that I will treasure. But most of all, I'll treasure the memory of this evening. I shall never forget you." She locked eyes with Michael. "Thank you for arranging this." She choked up, and Michael handed her his kerchief.

The other women, even Amelia, pulled out their handkerchiefs.

Simon chortled. "Buck up, ladies. You'll drown us with your tears."

Everyone laughed, restoring the lighthearted feeling of the evening, which lasted late into the night as they quitted the tavern and walked back to the wagon train. Anne, wrapped in the lingering pleasant memories of the evening, sat on a keg next to Amelia near the campfire.

They had not been seated long when someone called out, "Mr. Harrigan? Is Mr. Harrigan among you?"

"Here." Michael motioned to the man leading his mule to their campsite.

The animal was heavily laden with two ladder-back chairs

on one side, but in the dark, Anne could not make out what was strapped on the other side.

Michael helped the man untie the chairs that they placed on the ground near the fire. "I've grown tired of sitting on makeshift seats and the ground. And so..."

Amelia clapped her hands and plopped down on one of the chairs. "Brilliant idea."

Michael walked around the mule and loosened a rope, freeing a rocking chair that he placed in front of Anne. He bowed deeply as if to royalty. "Your throne awaits, my lady."

It was the very willow rocker Anne had sat in at the carpenter's shop. Her heart pounding, she huddled down into the chair and clasped the delicately curved arms.

"I am delighted beyond description. But it's too much."

"Nonsense. It's your birthday, and I had my orders from William to make it a merry one." He raised an eyebrow. "Have I succeeded?"

Anne pushed her feet against the ground and began to sway the chair back and forth. "Yes. William would be pleased. As am I." She relished the calm that came over her.

Soon, between the rocking, the ale, and the excitement of the day, her eyelids grew heavy, and her body melted into the high-backed *throne*. In her lethargy, she first heard Michael conversing with Amelia and then hammering.

The warmth of Michael's fingers tapping on her hand brought her to consciousness. "Time for bed," he whispered.

Fuzzy-headed, she stood. He circled her waist with his arm and led her toward her pallet.

"One last surprise," he murmured and helped her into a hammock.

She stretched out her legs, and the sides of the canvas enfolded her.

"No more sleeping on the ground." He tucked a coverlet around her. "Sleep well, my dearest friend."

The touch of his lips on her forehead sent warm waves through her exhausted body. She succumbed to sleep, but came to for a moment. Had he really kissed her, or had she dreamed it?

She snuggled down into the swaying cocoon. She would sort it out tomorrow.

CHAPTER 10

*T*he following week passed quickly with nothing out of the ordinary except for a river crossing. The churning water exhilarated Anne as she and Amelia stood beside their wagon on the raft that ferried them to the other side of a river swollen from a recent rain. Water splashed up onto the wooden planks and soaked her shoes and the hem of her petticoats. She pressed down on her straw hat that the whirling wind threatened to yank from her head. Careening over a wave, a corner of the raft dipped into the water. Two of their draft horses shied, but Michael settled them down and came to Anne's side.

Amelia tittered. "The arm muscles of the ferrymen pulling the rope are bulging. That one...there...looks as if he could break the barge pole in half."

Trust Amelia to note bulging muscles.

The guide ropes shuddered and grew taut.

Ignoring the threat of splinters, Anne gripped the rough, weathered railing. "Are those ropes strong enough to keep us from breaking free and floating downriver?"

The raft rocked, and Michael held her arm to steady her. "I'm sure they are. Not to worry."

Those words coming from Michael, as well as his honest expression, gave her all the assurance she needed.

One could get lost in those handsome, clear hazel eyes, today more green than brown.

As much as Anne enjoyed the ride across the river, she was relieved when the last wagon traversed it safely. The ordeal lasted most of the day, and the sun had begun to set. The clouds quickly changed from dark pink to crimson and purple. The country with its glorious sunsets, each one more spectacular than the last, had captured her heart.

"Circle the wagons in that clearing," Mr. Cooper yelled. "We've done enough for today."

Once they stopped, Michael tethered their horses to graze in a grassy area close by. He collected wood and started a fire, then placed the chairs and rocker on the stubby grass that had been beaten down by previous wagon trains.

Anne slumped into the rocker and stared at the campfire. She cherished her *throne* and took every opportunity to sit in it. Was it for the comfort, or because Michael had given it to her? Both.

"I'll need a couple of flat rocks for the teapot and frying pan," she said, reluctantly rising from the chair. "I'll search for some on the riverbank."

"I'll accompany you. It's not safe to go alone." Michael checked the pistol tucked into the waistband of his breeches.

He had removed his waistcoat. Sweat stained his shirt across his broad chest and under his armpits. Strands of his hair had come loose from the rawhide string and curled around his ears. Another man might look unkempt, but Michael stirred her senses.

They reached the bank and the water that had calmed considerably. She had picked her way to the edge and tapped a few rocks with her toe when a nearby bush rustled. A black furry creature no bigger than her hand waddled toward her.

"Aren't you a charming little thing," she said and bent down.

"No-o-o!" Michael spoke in a sharp, controlled whisper and grabbed her elbow. "Run, Anne. As fast as you can." The animal was hunching over and raising its tail.

Anne panicked. "Where?"

Michael glanced around. "Into the river and don't stop until the water covers your head." He pushed against the small of her back, guiding her. "You can swim?" he shouted and dropped his pistol onto the ground.

"N-no," she stammered. "What is it?"

Her heart hammered in her chest when, seconds later, she found herself floundering underneath the steady current. Michael grasped her waist and supported her as they both broke through the surface, gasping for air.

"What is it?" she asked again.

"Skunk."

She shook from head to toe. "I don't know what that is."

"You will in a moment."

She took a deep breath and inhaled the most horrible smell she had ever encountered. She grabbed her mobcap floating in the water and pressed it against her face.

"Skunks spray for protection, and it is the foulest stench. If it gets on you, it's almost impossible to wash away." He pointed upriver. "The wind is carrying the smell downriver, so let's go that way. I'll come back later for my pistol."

Michael curled his arm around her as they struggled against the current a few yards and then waded to the bank. He pulled on the hem of his shirt and sniffed and then he leaned over and sniffed her sleeve.

"What *are* you doing?" Shocked, she could hardly get the words out.

Michael's eyes danced, and he started chuckling. "Ha! I imagine my sniffing does seem a bit odd, but I don't think any of the spray got on us."

"Why are you laughing? I am drookit." She pulled at her skirts that clung to her legs and tried shaking out the water.

"Drookit?"

"Drenched," she answered through gritted teeth.

"Your face, Anne...when I told you to run. It's a picture I shall carry with me for a while." He chortled. "Come now, it was rather amusing." He cocked his head. "You don't have skunks where you are from?"

"No, we do not. Thank the heavens."

Anne let go of her irritation and started giggling. It set them off, and they laughed until she clutched her stomach. Suddenly, they grew quiet, and he stared at her intensely. Her pulse raced. He clasped her forearms and pulled her close enough to see the flecks of gold in his eyes and the lines in his full bottom lip.

"What are you two doing?" Amelia's strident voice shattered the intimate moment. "I heard your laughter from the wagon."

They quickly stepped back from each other.

Amelia strode toward them through the thin patch of woods that separated the riverbank from the campsite. She jammed her fists onto her hips. "Why are you both soaking wet?"

Anne wrung out her mobcap. "It's quite a story. But right now, I'd like to change out of these wet clothes." She glanced at Michael. "I'm sure Michael feels the same."

Back at their wagon, Michael waited beside the backboard while Anne climbed inside to change. She heard yelling and stood still.

"What is that horrible stench?" Eleanor shouted from across the campsite.

"It's a skunk," Simon bellowed.

"What's that?" Eleanor hollered back.

Wind had rushed up from the river and had wafted the odor toward the far end of the circled wagons.

A giggle erupted inside of Anne, and she burst out laughing. Michael's deep-throated chortle echoed from the other side of the canvas, sealing a bond between them.

She closed her eyes and recalled Michael standing on the riverbank, throwing back his head and laughing so hard, his barrel chest shook with it. What a pleasant memory. The next moment, a vision of Michael's lips so close to hers overshadowed that memory, igniting a fire in the pit of her stomach.

In the coming days, the bond altered something between them and intensified Anne's awareness of Michael's every move. It altered Amelia's behavior as well. She no longer batted her eyes or simpered around Michael.

She approached Anne about it one evening while Michael tended the horses. "You have a heart for him, don't you?"

"As a friend." Anne avoided eye contact.

It was not a complete lie.

Amelia scoffed. "As you please."

Amelia had ferreted out Anne's true feelings. Did Michael suspect? The man was still in love with his wife. Did he compare Anne with her? How much did she fall short in that comparison? Did he even think about her at all, except as a *dear friend*?

How painful it was loving someone who did not return that love. What was she to do?

The journey ahead changed into a path of eggshells over which she must tread lightly, guarding her heart and hiding her feelings.

CHAPTER 11

"*H*ow much longer until we leave the train, Michael?" Amelia, sitting on the wagon seat beside him, cooled her face with a fan. "It's close to evening, and it's still dreadfully hot. Almost unbearable. I thought you said it would get cooler in the mountains."

Michael tightened the reins around his hands. "About a week till the turnoff to Graniteville. And, yes, it's hot. It is cooler today than yesterday and will get cooler the higher up we travel."

Amelia's incessant complaining wore on Michael, and he was hard-pressed to curtail his grumpiness. Thank heavens Anne maintained her calm demeanor. How would one contend with two bad-tempered women?

They were stationed near the tail end of the train, and dust from the wagons ahead whirled in the air. Anne coughed several times.

Michael swiveled toward her. "We'll break for supper soon. Are you sure you don't want to come sit with us?"

Anne shot him a sideways glance. "I'm sure."

What a glare Anne gave him. Had he done something to raise her hackles?

Mr. Connor rode up and down the train shouting for drivers to turn their wagons into a clearing up ahead. Once Michael maneuvered their wagon into a circle with the others, he tethered and fed the horses. After he placed their chairs on the grass, Amelia plopped down in one of them while Anne gathered wood at the edge of the trees.

"I'll start the fire, Anne." Michael moved forward and nearly missed being knocked in his shin from a piece of kindling that flew out from a pile she had slammed to the ground.

Anne was riled. Why was she glaring at him? So much for being calm.

"I appreciate that *someone* among us is willing to help." Anne jammed a fist onto her hip.

Amelia shot up from her chair. "Is that remark a slant towards me, Anne Forbes?"

Anne stiffened her back. "Yes. I was speakin' of you, Amelia Stanford. And while I'm slantin', may I say, Michael, you need to step up."

Why were they so waspish, and why was Anne speaking with a Scottish brogue? Completely perplexed by the heightened friction in the air, Michael kept silent.

"Please, Michael, tell her that you hired me as a chaperone, not a maid," Anne snapped. "It's no' fair that I have been made to take on the lion's share of work."

Amelia tucked in her chin. "Please, Michael, remind Anne that I have been gravely ill and that I lost my best friend."

"I acknowledge that, but she has almost fully recovered and is able to take on some responsibilities. I would have you remind her, Michael, that it was I who nursed her through her illness." Anne's lips quivered. "And I lost my darling, precious nephew."

Anne shook so hard, Michael would not have been surprised if rockets shot out from her mobcap. He remained stock still, amazed at this new side of her. Being stuck in the middle between two very angry women was quickly becoming uncomfortable. How best to handle this extremely unfamiliar territory?

"Ladies...and let's remember that you *are* ladies..." He had not intended to sound so pompous. Their shocked faces registered agreement. He must take another approach. "Amelia, you should help out more. You seem well enough. Anne, can you think of some light duties for her?"

Amelia wrapped her arms around her waist and began to cry.

Anne hurried to her and hugged her. "Look what you've done. You've made Amelia cry. You didn't have to be so ungentleman-like." Her voice broke, and she started to cry.

"Don't cry, dear Anne," Amelia said through her sniffles. "He can't help being a lout. He is a man, after all."

The scene playing out before Michael stunned him. "I beg your pardon. I resent being called a lout. I cannot recall a single word I said that was ungentleman-like!"

Anne tried to dry Amelia's tears with her kerchief and then brandished it at him. "Dunno yell at us, Michael Harrigan."

What was occurring, and why was everyone using their full names?

"I did not yell, but I can see I have been made a villain in this piece." He grabbed his pistol and shoved it into his waistband. "I shall withdraw."

What had he done to deserve their mistreatment of him? Nothing. Is this what he had to look forward to?

*A*nne flounced down onto her rocking chair and pushed the ground with her toes, rocking back and forth.

Sniffling, Amelia sat beside her. "He will come back, won't he?"

"Of that I'm certain." Anne slowed her rocking. "Though we did give him a difficult time when he has done nothing wrong."

As Amelia wiped her eyes with her handkerchief, guilt rode high over Anne's thoughts.

"I am sorry I was so cross with you." She stopped rocking. "I have been thinking of my family, my nephew, my choice to travel on to Graniteville. I was overcome with grief and doubt and...fear. Emotions which plague you as well, I'm sure." She faced Amelia. "It struck me that I don't know much about you. Only that you were Megan's longtime friend and that you grew up together in Scotland."

Amelia perked up. "We grew up together in England until both our families moved to Scotland when we were thirteen. Same as you, as I recall. "

Anne nodded.

"We were cousins, you see. Our fathers were brothers. But we were more like sisters. Both our mothers and fathers died of influenza when we had recently turned sixteen, and it was determined that we would both live with a distant relative." Amelia chuckled. "Poor Aunt Agatha, a spinster—she was quite nonplused having to manage two young girls on the brink of womanhood."

There was that word—*spinster*. Anne had taken over from Aunt Agatha.

"On her eighteenth birthday, Megan met Cal."

"What was Cal doing in Scotland?"

"He was exploring sawmills in England and Scotland. He had heard about a mill in Leith...where Megan and I lived...

that was driven by a windmill." Amelia shook her head. "Anyway, they married within weeks of meeting. Cal was five years older than Megan, utterly charming, and extremely handsome." She sighed. "Much like his brother."

Anne glanced at Michael conversing with Simon a few wagons away. Cal truly must be handsome. Michael's back was ramrod stiff, and he seemed agitated. Poor man—she and Amelia had been harsh with him.

"I was bereft when Megan moved to the colonies. But she left me with a promise to return and bring me back here with her. Almost two years passed until she came back to Scotland to help me settle Aunt Agatha's estate. The dear woman left everything to us, making me a fine prospect, as they say." She studied her hands resting in her lap. "Now my dearest friend has gone, along with all of our plans."

Amelia's forlorn expression touched Anne's heart, and she reached over and clasped her hand. "I would hope that you would consider me your friend."

Tears welled in Amelia's eyes, and she laced her fingers through Anne's. "I should like that so very much."

Anne observed Michael a few minutes. He kept his back to her. Was he still angry? "I feel we must do something to atone for our behavior towards Michael."

"Did I truly call him a lout?"

"I called him ungentleman-like."

They looked at each other and burst into giggles.

~

*T*horoughly confused and quite disconcerted by the confrontation with Anne and Amelia, Michael had stomped away and joined Simon at his wagon. They spent the evening discussing the vagaries of women.

Michael poked the campfire with a stick. "It was as if I had come upon two porcupines in full array of their quills."

Simon adjusted his spectacles that remained perched on his forehead more often than his nose. "Tut. Tut. I dare say it must have been surprising."

"*Surprising* is an understatement. First, their waspishness toward one another. Then the crying. And then the darts thrown my way." Michael pushed a coal back into the flames. "No one has ever called me a lout. The crying was bad enough, but the accusation of me acting ungentleman-like was truly unfair."

Simon drew on his pipe, circling smoke around his bald head. "They said those things? Women. Can one ever fathom what they are thinking and why?"

As the night wore on, Michael became convinced that the cordwainer, a confirmed bachelor, was unable to shed any light on the situation, except that women were akin to close-fitting shoes...very uncomfortable.

Thinking it safe to return to his campsite, Michael made his way quietly to the wagon. Anne and Amelia slept in their hammocks. A plate of biscuits and ham sat on a rock, kept warm by the fire. When he finished eating his supper, he found that his pallet had been laid underneath the wagon and cushioned with sweet-smelling pine boughs.

A truce?

Lying on his pallet with his arms folded under his head, Michael said his bedtime prayer that ended with, *Dear Lord, give me grace to bear what tomorrow brings.*

CHAPTER 12

*T*he altercation changed each of them. Michael watched his words closely, unwilling to be called ungentleman-like ever again, while to his astonishment, Anne and Amelia conversed and laughed together often.

Two days later after supper, the three of them sat in their chairs watching the others settle down for the night when a single wagon carrying a man and a woman pulled off the road and into the clearing. Michael kept watch on the driver as he guided his two horses in a circle and stopped facing out toward the trail. Instead of a canvas bonnet, the wagon's rounded roof was fashioned of wood. Sunflower-yellow trim edged its green-and-red-striped sides. The wood of the double-paned glass door was intricately carved with trees and vines.

"What an odd-looking wagon. Who are they?" Amelia craned her neck.

Michael reached under his chair for his pistol. "They call their wagon a *vardo*, and they are Romani...gypsies."

Anne edged forward on her rocker. "I've seen people like them before. A caravan came through our town in Scotland. Although they didn't bother anyone, when they had left, some townspeople complained about missing farm tools and livestock."

They left their wagon and joined other wagoners gathered around the strange-looking couple.

The wagon master conversed with the visitors and then approached Michael. "They asked if they could feed and water their horses and possibly stay the night. I gave permission, but I'm ordering Sanders to keep an eye on them. I'm not sure I like the looks of them."

Michael nodded. "It's best to be cautious."

The driver jumped down from the wagon seat and bowed to the crowd. The full sleeves of his shirt billowed in the breeze. Its open neck exposed his chest. Too much chest, in Michael's opinion.

"Good evening, ladies and gentlemen. We are Mr. and Mrs. Boswell, and we can't thank you enough for your hospitality."

"I wonder where the fabric of his breeches came from," Anne said in a lowered voice. "Wide brown stripes on a gold background. I've never seen the like."

The man's wife handed him a concertina before accepting his assistance to dismount.

"My goodness," Anne said, studying the woman's clothing. "Look at the intricate pattern in her blouse and the coins sewn into her belt sash. I believe her skirt is silk. I should like a closer look."

Amelia leaned toward Anne. "The fringe on her shawl must be two feet long."

Michael snorted. Leave it to the ladies to comment on fashion.

Mr. Boswell slipped his hands into the straps of the instrument, stretched it out, and pushed it back together. "In payment, may we provide you with some entertainment?"

He had played only a few bars of a lively tune before Eleanor and Oliver Tanner started clapping their hands and tapping their toes. The Daniels brothers and their wives formed up for a country dance, and soon others joined in.

Michael held back while Anne and Amelia, giggling like children and caught up in the merriment, lined up, circling and linking arms with the other couples.

How different the women behaved after their argument. The squabble had spurred a sweet friendship. Michael vowed never again to find himself the subject of their combined wrath.

Anne's wide smile and lighthearted movements lifted his spirits, and he started tapping his toes and clapping. Someone should ensure she had more joy in her life.

As the evening wore on, the wagoners either danced or sang along with Mr. Boswell's playing. Anne's playfulness was infectious, but try as she might to get Michael to dance, he begged off. He had never enjoyed dancing, even with Heather, and she loved dancing more than eating. The memory of her circling with others, stepping lively in a country dance...her petticoats swaying...her face a picture of loveliness...jabbed his heart.

The night wore on, and the group slowly dispersed. When they returned to the wagon, Anne shuffled through the material she had placed on a keg near her rocker. She started frantically searching the ground around the keg.

"Is something amiss?" Michael asked.

"My shears. They are gone. I know I left them here." Anne wrung her hands. "They were special ordered from Sheffield and cost me dearly."

Hackles played across Michael's back. "The gypsies."

Anne frowned. "But they were with us the entire time."

Michael stomped toward the Boswells' wagon, where the couple fed hay to their horses.

"Do be careful. I cannot have you harmed over a pair of shears," Anne called out.

At the back of the vardo, Michael pounded on the door with his pistol handle. "Come out. I know someone is in there."

All remained silent.

"Come out, or I'll come in," Michael shouted.

The door slammed open, and a man lunged out and hurtled into Michael, throwing him to the ground and tossing the pistol yards away. Startled, Michael took several blows to his head before he rallied, grabbed his assailant by his shoulders, and tossed him off. His left eye blurred, and he felt blood running down his cheek. Angrier than he had been in a long time, he jumped on top of the man and pummeled him.

Mr. Boswell grabbed Michael from behind, but Mr. Cooper shoved him away and drew his pistol. "Stop!" he yelled. "What's going on?"

The Boswells helped the battered man to his feet and supported him between them.

His breath coming in ragged spurts, Michael stood and bent over, resting his hands on his knees. "I'm certain that this man, while Boswells distracted us, was stealing from us." He sucked in a deep breath and picked up his pistol. "Look in the wagon. I think you'll find shears belonging to Miss Forbes. And possibly other stolen items."

Mr. Cooper waved his gun at the Boswells and their accomplice. "Move over there, to your horses. Mr. Sanders, search the wagon."

The scout shuffled around inside, came out, and dumped the contents of a satchel on the ground. Several of the wagoners who had watched the fight sifted through the loot.

"Here are the shears." Simon brandished the scissors. "And here are my hammer and awl."

Michael handed the shears to Anne, now huddled with Amelia next to him.

"Are you all right?" she murmured, her brown eyes anxious.

He patted her arm and wiped the blood from his eye. "I'm fine, Anne." He snorted. "Though a little worse for wear."

Amelia frowned. "Don't make light of it, Michael. It looks serious. More than just a scratch."

"That's my wife's cameo." Mr. Tanner swept up the pin and slipped it into his waistcoat. "You dirty thief." He raised a fist at the man, who cowered.

Mr. Cooper pointed his pistol at the gypsies. "That's it. You'd best leave...and fast."

The gypsies scrambled around and quickly headed out from the campsite.

Watching the wagon make the turn onto the trail, Michael felt Anne's cold fingers curl around his.

"Come with me." She tugged his arm. "Let me tend to you."

At their wagon, Michael sat in a chair while Anne examined the gash in his forehead at his hairline. She moved in so closely, her breath fanned his cheek. A faint aroma of lavender wafted about her. Hadn't he smelled it once before when they first met? It suited her—fresh, appealing, sweet.

"It will take a stitch, maybe two." She stepped back and stared into his eyes. "May I? It will hurt, and I don't have anything to dull the pain."

What a genuinely caring person. His Heather had been the same.

"I trust you. And don't worry about the pain."

"I'll fetch a pail of water and some cloths," Amelia offered.

When Amelia returned, Anne gathered needle and thread and her medicine kit. With a touch as light as a frond of fir, she washed away the blood from the wound and his face. Biting down on the corner of her lip, she pressed open the torn skin, and he winced.

Amelia, watching close by, grimaced but remained silent.

"I am sorry." Anne dropped the soiled cloth into the pail. "But I had to make sure there was no dirt. Everything must be clean before I sew it together."

Michael studied her face. "You've done this before."

Her expression became thoughtful. "Many times. My da was prone to accidents. Once my skill with a needle became apparent, repairing his wounds became my responsibility."

"How old were you when they discovered your skill?"

She punched the thread through the eye of a needle. "About eight, I think."

No wonder Anne was so proficient. She had learned responsibility at a very early age. He admired her even more.

She stepped in between his knees, leaned forward, and tilted his chin up with the tip of her finger. "Brace yourself. I'm starting now."

It would take little effort to embrace her. A sharp, stinging pain halted that thought and brought tears to his eyes.

"One more to go." She gently pushed back a strand of his hair.

The gesture gave him time to take in a deep breath and prepare for the next stitch that hurt as much as the first.

"Done." She opened a tin from her medicine kit and gingerly applied ointment to the wound. Tying off the knot of the strip of gauze she had secured around his temple, she asked, "Would you like a cup of tea?"

Michael blew out a deep breath and shook his head. Between the wound and Anne's closeness, he required something much stronger than tea.

That evening, as he lay on his pallet gazing up at the stars that shone like diamonds on black velvet, Michael remembered the smell and feel of Anne...the gentle touch of her fingers on his face. What would it be like to wrap his arms around her? Not for comfort as he had done before. But for pleasure. Would it be as delightful as holding his Heather had been?

CHAPTER 13

*A*fter traveling three hundred miles in almost two months, Anne could barely contain her excitement when Michael guided the horses off the road leading to Graniteville and onto the town's main thoroughfare.

Had it been only a week since she had said farewell to the wagoners who had become dear friends? The women had wept and hugged and promised to write one another, while the men shook hands and clapped each other on their backs. Mr. Cooper, pressing his tricorn to his chest, thanked Anne once again for her assistance during the smallpox tragedy and professed he did not know what they would have done without her. Letting go of Eleanor Tanner distressed Anne the most. She had come to love the dear woman. Before leaving their separate ways, the wagoners had formed a circle, and Mr. Cooper had led them in a prayer beseeching the Lord for safe travels and blessings on their new endeavors.

The seven-day trek from that point on had progressed smoothly. Anne and Amelia's relationship deepened as, each day, nature laid out before them glorious prospects—spectacular sunrises and sunsets, valleys spattered with wildflowers of every color imaginable, gurgling streams and creeks with water as cold as ice, sweet-smelling cedars, and impressive boulders striated with glistening minerals.

Michael, obviously proud and pleased with their response to his mountains, took every opportunity to point out the array of wildlife, including a herd of bison with their magnificent triangle-shaped faces, black beards, and hunched, furry backs.

For the past few miles of their trek, Anne and Amelia had sat on either side of him as the narrow, rocky mountain roads made walking beside the wagon difficult.

The first sight of the town in the midmorning sunshine made Anne gasp. "It's even more beautiful than you described."

Rows of dogwood trees that had recently shed their blooms grew on both sides of the street. Pristine buildings in all shapes and sizes formed rows—a cooper, a sheriff's office, a potter, a schoolhouse, a bakery, and a blacksmith and livery. Some shops had placed clay pots at their entrances, which were filled with flowers of a myriad colors. Two of them Anne recognized as fiery red-flame azaleas and purple phlox.

"Look." Anne pointed to the largest log building with a porch across the front. "It's a mercantile. I do hope they keep a supply of material and notions."

A white clapboard church with its spire reaching toward the brilliant blue sky stood as a bastion at the edge of town. Behind it, row upon row of azure mountains rolled into the distance, as if God had raised a blue satin coverlet and let it settle to the bedrock below.

Anne filled her lungs with a huge breath of fresh air, and suddenly, a part of her that had lain dormant came alive. "Michael, it's stunning."

"I knew you would like it. I've lived here my entire life, and the sight of the mountains never fails to fill me with awe."

"The town is rather quaint," Amelia commented.

Anne poked Amelia's side. "Rather quaint? You do know how to make an understatement."

Michael winked.

Anne leaned to the side and studied the road's surface, bits of which reflected the sunlight here and there. "What is the covering on the road? It's strange to me."

"It's crushed granite. We have an abundance of rain and snow in the winter here. The granite helps keep the mud down." He pulled back on the reins and slowed the horses. "There's a granite mine close. You'll see houses made of it, like this one." He motioned to a two-story dwelling constructed of dark-gray stones. A shingle hung over the door which read, *Clarendon Boarding House.* "This is where I plan for you and Amelia to stay."

Amelia scooted to the edge of the seat and stared at the house. "We're not staying with you?"

"Cal and I are both widowers...now." He paused. "It would not be proper."

Michael's expression was grim. Was he pondering the difficult task of telling his brother about Megan's death? He was one of the strongest men Anne had ever known. Yet she wished she could ease his burden.

He maneuvered the horses off the main street and onto a wide path leading around to the back of the granite house. He brought the horses to a stop, wrapped the reins around the brake, slid past Amelia, and stepped down. He held out his arms to her, and she jumped, landing against his chest. Before Michael could reach Anne, she descended using the wooden steps nailed into the wagon bed. She scanned the lush garden that encompassed the entire back yard. Flowers blanketed part of the space. The other part flourished with melons, cabbages, and turnips. Two rows burgeoned with corn, bean vines growing up the stalks and squash plants at the base.

Michael pointed to the corn. "The Cherokee taught us how

to grow it that way. They call it *three sisters*. The stalks provide
the beans support, and the squash plants nourish the soil and
help keep the bugs away."

"There are Indians close by?" asked Anne.

"Yes. Several villages. I count many Cherokee among my
friends. If it weren't for their help, I don't think the settlers who
established Graniteville would have survived."

She shook her head. "I have so much to learn."

"I'll help you, Anne."

As a friend? As a spinster old enough to hire as a chaperone
for a younger woman?

Amelia grabbed Michael's forearm. "Who is that?"

A tall, slender, elderly woman descended the steps of the
back porch and hurried toward them. "Michael, it's so very
good to see you. You've been away too long." She stared a
moment at Amelia's grasp on Michael's arm and then cocked
her head toward Anne.

Despite the wrinkles on her face and the wisps of gray
hair peeking out from her mobcap, she exuded an aura of
liveliness. Her lovely petunia-blue eyes sparkled with
keenness.

Michael moved away from Amelia's hold on him. "Iris, may
I introduce you to Miss Anne Forbes and Miss Amelia Stanford? Ladies, this is Mrs. Iris Clarendon."

The ladies curtsied to one another.

Mrs. Clarendon glanced at the wagon. "Where is Megan?"

Michael cleared his throat. "Our wagon train was struck
with smallpox. Megan passed away."

Mrs. Clarendon shook her head. "Tragic. She was a beautiful woman. Poor Cal will be devastated."

"Amelia, Megan's girlhood friend, wanted to continue her
journey here. Anne graciously agreed to serve as her
companion."

Mrs. Clarendon looked from Anne to Amelia and back.

"That must make for an interesting story. I look forward to making your acquaintance."

"Do you have rooms to accommodate them?" asked Michael.

"I do." Mrs. Clarendon motioned toward the wagon. "Their luggage?"

"Six trunks...only two for Anne...four for Amelia as well as several hat boxes." Michael rolled his eyes.

Mrs. Clarendon's eyes sparkled with humor. "I'll take the ladies to their accommodations and send the boys out to assist you."

Upstairs, Anne paused in the doorway of her chamber. The wide planks of the dark hardwood floors shone and smelled of beeswax. A four-poster bed with a dark-blue coverlet faced a fireplace with a mantel of the same wood as the floor. A vanity and chair sat in one corner, and a ceiling-high wardrobe dominated the opposite wall. A vase filled with blue phlox sat atop a washstand next to a cream-colored porcelain pitcher and bowl.

Anne clapped her hands. "It's delightful."

Amelia hovered with Mrs. Clarendon in the hallway. "It is pleasant enough."

Anne sighed. "There you go again, Amelia, with your understatements."

A gust of wind wafted through the open window and billowed the curtains that matched the bed coverlet.

Anne pushed aside the curtains. "A view of the blue mountains. What a fine prospect. I shall enjoy waking to this sight in the mornings. I couldn't be more pleased, Mrs. Clarendon. May I place my rocking chair just here...until I find a place of my own? Michael purchased it for me at one of the settlements we visited."

"Of course." The woman fluttered her hand. "I'm happy that you like the room. And, both of you, please, you must call me

Iris." She motioned down the hall. "Amelia, let me show you to your room."

A half hour later, Anne was hanging dresses in the wardrobe when Michael paused in the open doorway. He had rolled up his sleeves, exposing the dark hair on his tanned arms. Sweat shone on his forehead, and tendrils of wet hair clung to the sides of his face. Her heart fluttered.

"It's to your liking?" His eager expression was endearing.

"I could not want for more. It's beyond lovely. Thank you for bringing me here."

He grinned. "Now that you and Amelia are settling in, I'll be on my way."

He was leaving. The thought raked across her heart.

"I'll be back to check on you...and Amelia. And Cal and I will want you to join us for dinner another time. You'll like Cal, I'm sure. And I want to introduce you to Cate."

Anne looked forward to meeting Michael's daughter and making a dress for her. How would the young girl react when she saw the materials for her new Sunday outfit?

"I'm eager to meet them both, though I understand it may be a while in remembrance of Megan."

"Yes." He furrowed his brow. "I'll leave you to it, then." He strode down the hallway.

Michael had shown concern for her comfort despite the heavy burden he bore of breaking the news to his brother about his wife's death. What a terribly sad task awaited him.

His absence created a painful void.

$\sim$

*L*ater, after Anne and Amelia had shared afternoon tea with Iris, Amelia begged off to take a nap.

"You are not tired, Anne?" Iris covered the teapot

with a cozy decorated with pansies the color of Iris's bodice and petticoats.

Anne folded her arms on the table situated in front of a window looking out on the town's main thoroughfare. "I'm too excited. Everything is so new, and I don't know what to explore first."

A servant girl entered and started to take away the tea tray.

"Anne, this is Helen. She'll be happy to assist you with requests you may have."

"Hello, Helen. It's a pleasure to meet you."

"My pleasure, ma'am." Helen curtsied before gathering the tea tray and leaving.

Anne appreciated her pleasant demeanor and stark white starched apron. Looking around, she felt at home in the comfortable room decorated in shades of green and turquoise. Two settees faced each other next to a fireplace decorated with blue-and-white tiles depicting scenes of an English country-side. The portrait of a robust, red-haired man dressed in tartans hung over the mantel.

Anne motioned to the painting. "What a handsome man."

"That's my husband, Mathew." Iris's face fairly glowed. The expression of a woman who had loved deeply.

"How long have you had the boarding house?"

"Going on ten years, since my Mathew passed. This was originally our home. Mathew built it himself."

"It's an impressive building. Sturdy. I can imagine it still standing a hundred years from now. It will be a fine legacy."

Iris gazed out the window, her expression wistful. "It will be our only legacy, I fear. God did not bless us with children."

Anne remained silent. Was it God's plan for her to marry and have children?

"Anyway, you may wonder why there aren't more boarders." Iris folded her hands in her lap. "I don't need the income. My Mathew left me quite comfortable. I take in patrons only when it pleases me and I'm in want of company. I do have some regular visitors, especially in the fall when our trees turn the most magnificent colors, rivaling our brilliant sunsets." Enthusiasm lit her face. "How one can view such splendor and not believe in God, I cannot fathom. I simply cannot wait for you to experience it."

"You make it sound glorious. I look forward to it."

Iris leaned forward and put her hand on Anne's hand that rested on her knee. "So...I have to know how you came about acting as a...companion."

"It's quite a long story."

"We have time. Do we not?" Iris settled back in her chair.

As Anne unfolded her account of the past few months, Iris's beautifully expressive face changed from excitement for the journey, to horror for the smallpox victims, to grief for Keith's and Megan's deaths, to admiration for Anne's choice to become a proprietor of her own tailor shop.

"You have lived more in these past months than some experience in a lifetime. I admire you, Anne, and as sure as I am sitting here, I know we will be the best of friends."

The woman's sweet declaration warmed Anne. "I should like that very much."

Iris, her bones popping slightly, rose from her chair and held out her hand. "I think I can assist you to fulfill one part of your dream."

"What?"

"Let's not talk about it until we get there." Iris's eyes glowed with her secret. "If you're up to a short walk, I will show you."

Out on the street, they moved toward the entrance to the town and had traversed only a couple of blocks when they stopped in front of a two-story clapboard building. The placard overhead read *Bakery*. Iris retrieved a key from her underpocket and unlocked the glass-paned double doors. Full of curiosity, Anne followed her inside.

Iris whirled around. "What do you think? Will it do?"

It took a moment for Anne to realize what she asked.

Tingling from head to toe, Anne explored the two rooms that comprised the shop. Overlooking the dust, abandoned sacks of flour, pots and pans, overturned chairs, and the long wooden bread peel standing in the corner, she immediately recognized the shop's potential. "It's perfect. How do I acquire information about it?"

Iris grinned. "Me. I'm the owner."

Anne's heart leapt. Maybe...just maybe...her prayers would come true. The Lord had been guiding her path all along.

"The baker who rented the shop from me ran off months ago when he heard a rumor that gold had been discovered in the northwest corner of the Georgia colony. I would be thrilled to sell or rent it to you. But before you decide, let me show you a lovely surprise."

She took Anne by her elbow and guided her into the back room and up a flight of stairs. When they reached a landing at the top, Iris opened a door that led into a cozy apartment. "Thankfully, this part was kept fairly clean."

Her heart thumping madly, Anne wandered around the room, touching the bed, the mantel, and a small table and chair. She gazed out the window and, to her utmost delight, discovered an awe-inspiring view of row upon row of cedar trees climbing up the side of a mountain. The setting sun had colored the tops of the evergreens a brilliant orange-red as if they were on fire.

Anne could not stop shaking. "It is beautiful...beyond anything I could have imagined. So beautiful, in fact, I'm hesitant to ask the price."

Iris hugged her. "We will speak of price later. For now, dry those lovely eyes, my dear. There's much to be done."

CHAPTER 14

*M*ichael and Cal settled into chairs on the front of the L-shaped porch of their house. Their hound dog, Bramble, stretched out between them, already asleep after an early-morning jaunt. The golden rays of sunrise painted the tops of the cedar trees that climbed up the mountain across from the valley that was their front yard. They sat in the ladder-backs Michael had purchased while on the wagon train. Cal knocked his pipe against his boot, dumping out the spent ashes. He unbuttoned the pocket of his tan canvas shirt and tucked in the pipe.

"I wonder if she's sitting in the rocker," Michael mumbled.

Cal leaned back his chair and tightened the rawhide string that secured his shoulder-length hair. Though his hair was the same dark hue as Michael's, he wore his longer. "Who?"

Michael tucked in his chin, startled that he had spoken the words aloud. "Anne."

"Oh...Anne." Cal snorted. "You've been home only three days, and I have lost count of the number of times I've heard her name."

"Don't tease me about her. I made it possible for her to come to Graniteville. So, naturally, I feel responsible for her."

Cal's eyes danced. "Naturally."

Was his brother being sarcastic? Michael pursed his lips. "She truly is a many-faceted person. Did I tell you about the time we met with a skunk?"

"No. You told me about how ably she handled the smallpox. How beautifully she sews and the way she cared for her brother and his family, and how lovely her voice—"

"You'll like this one, Cal. I haven't laughed as hard in quite some time."

"This I have to hear."

"We were beside a river looking for flat rocks to use for cooking by the fire, when out from the bushes waddles a baby skunk."

"Uh-oh."

"Uh-oh is right. Well, Anne had never seen a skunk. Didn't know what it was. She started to pet it when I yelled for her to run into the water. You should have seen her face, Cal." He snorted. "Running knee-deep, I asked if she knew how to swim, and she shouted that she didn't. Anyway, with me holding onto her, we ducked all the way under the water and stayed there until I thought it was safe. When we came up, I realized that the skunk had sprayed. We waded upriver and came out soaked to the skin. The wind sent the stench into the camp, and we could hear people yelling, wondering what that terrible smell was. We started laughing and kept on until we cried."

Cal chortled. "That's quite a story."

"I know. It amazes me that she didn't know what a skunk is."

Cal's expression sobered. "It amazes *me* that she trusted you so much, she ran into water over her head without knowing how to swim."

Michael rubbed his chin. "That never occurred to me."

He pondered the thought a few moments. Anne had put

her trust in him many times since their first meeting. It humbled him. Perhaps she regarded him more than he realized.

He stood and leaned against a porch post. "I heard from one of the men that she's renting the old bakery from Iris."

Cal crossed his ankles. "I'm surprised you haven't gone to see about her yourself."

Michael gripped the railing. "I know. I thought it best to give her breathing room. Time to settle in. She'll have much to think about and many decisions to make. I'm certain that Iris is taking care of her...providing guidance."

"It's going to take a lot of work to make it into a decent shop." Michael whirled around. "We won't be busy at the mill for another month. Should I send a couple of our men to help her?"

Cal rose from the chair with a groan and rubbed his sore leg. He rested his hand on Michael's shoulder. "It would be a kind, neighborly thing to do. And, as you say, the men aren't that busy."

The sunrise had painted the sky myriad shades of orange and yellow. Bramble yawned and stretched and waddled over to the top of the porch steps.

"I'm not teasing you now when I say this...and I've not even met Anne, but could she mean more to you than you're willing to admit? It's been nine years since Heather died. Do you think it's time to move on with your life? If nothing else, Caitlin needs a mother. She spends too much time in the kitchen with Cookie and roaming the forest with Bramble."

"There is a connection between us. Many times, I've felt an urge to hold her, and not only for comfort. I miss her when she isn't close by. But I fear she only sees me as a friend. Someone who has shown her kindness." Michael stroked his beard. "An impression I may have had a hand in as many times as I called her *friend*."

"She does seem to occupy your thoughts. And many successful marriages have been based on friendship." Cal frowned. "Would that Megan and I had possessed such a foundation."

Michael faced his brother. "I apologize. Here I've been rattling on about Anne, when you are grieving your wife."

"I am deeply saddened by her passing. But, if I'm honest, ours was not a good match. Megan hated it here. When we married in Scotland, I believe she thought we would live in a place like Philadelphia, not in some remote settlement with no genteel society to speak of. It became apparent early on that I was a disappointment."

"No, you mustn't say that. In Megan's last moments, she spoke of you with love. She regretted that she had not been a better wife to you."

The relief in Cal's eyes tugged Michael's heart.

Would he and Anne make a good match? Considering it shook him to his core. Visions of her flashed through his mind —laughing heartily over their narrow escape from the skunk, the blue smudges under her eyes from caring for the sick, the way her glasses magnified her fine brown eyes, the feel of her in his embrace. Deep, profound sensations flooded his body. Elation, astonishment, yearning, and hope stirred his blood, but the most disturbing was fear. He never again wanted to suffer losing someone he loved more than his own life.

Did he love Anne in such a way? He believed so. But he must tread carefully. She poised on the brink of a new life that would give her the independence she craved. Would not marriage stifle that? Could his pride give way for a self-reliant wife?

He vowed to seek answers to those questions...and soon.

CHAPTER 15

$\mathcal{F}$our days passed after her arrival in Graniteville before Anne stood outside her shop. *Her shop.* She could barely contain her excitement.

Drafting and signing the business agreement had taken two days, although it would not be complete until Michael signed as her appointed male representative.

Why had he not come to see her? There could be many reasons—maybe he comforted his brother, or maybe he had to catch up on his business he had been away from for months, or he might be spending time with his daughter. Whatever the explanation, Anne missed him terribly.

Iris had insisted Anne take a couple of days to explore and to sleep, deeply snuggled in the downy-filled mattress so different from the ground and hammock she had endured on the trail.

As she unlocked the shop door, she recalled her time familiarizing herself with the town and its people.

Mr. Hale, the proprietor of the mercantile and tea shop, had greeted her warmly. They discussed the need for the store to increase its inventory of fabric. Her own minimal supply would play out soon, and she needed assurance that her patrons could find the materials they desired from the mercantile.

At the pottery, she purchased a vase to set outside her store entrance. It would match those in front of all the other main street stores. She had already planned to fill it with pink mountain laurels that reminded her of porcelain.

She had checked in with Mr. Drayton, the carpenter. His supply of ladder-back chairs and finely crafted furniture amazed her. More amazing was his array of guitars, dulcimers, and mandolins. He had crafted them all from wood Michael supplied.

Visiting the blacksmith reminded her of Eleanor and Oliver Tanner and their birthday gift of a whetstone. She cherished the memory of that lovely surprise party and the laughter she shared with her friends.

Would she ever see the Tanners or any of the others again? They had promised to write, but they would all be busy establishing their new lives. Drawing close to and loving people who had circled in and then out of her life made her melancholy.

She had sat a while with the sheriff outside his small constabulary. He had never had a run-in with any serious criminals, only the occasional man who had imbibed too much on a Saturday evening. With his gray hair and beard and watery blue eyes, he exuded confidence that gave Anne a sense of security.

Other businesses awaited her, but for now, it was her time. Her business. Once inside, she twirled around in the front room and made a quick, sobering inventory. The place was well and truly a mess. Layers of dust and cobwebs covered objects scattered around the rooms. The dust accumulated so thick in places, it rendered some things unrecognizable.

Where to start?

In the back room, she placed her satchel atop a huge work

table in front of the fireplace, then pinned an apron top to her bodice and tied the streamers around her waist. She picked up a mop and broom and banged them against a table leg, showering a cloud of dust around her.

Sneezing and coughing, she grabbed a kerchief from the satchel and formed a mask that covered her nose and mouth. She had worked only a half hour when a knock sounded at the double front doors she had left ajar. She pulled the mask down around her neck and hurried to the entrance, where she was greeted by two tall, muscular, and heavily bearded men wearing red-and-black-checked shirts, canvas breeches, and knee-length boots. Their brown eyes and handsome features favored each other. Brothers?

"Yes?" She wiped her hands on her apron.

The taller of the two removed his hat. "Miss Forbes?"

"I am."

"If I may introduce us...I'm Sam Craig, and this is my cousin Mark Gibbons."

They bowed and she curtsied.

"We finished delivering a load of basswood to the carpenter, and Mr. Harrigan, our employer, told us to stop by to see if we could lend you a hand. Especially if you have large items that need hauling away."

"Well, um..." She glanced over her shoulder. "I could use some help."

Bless Michael. Even in his absence, he had found a way to support her.

The young men, their expressions eager, followed her inside and through to the back room.

"The first thing I need is to see if the fireplaces work. The one here and the one upstairs. Please, make sure there are no obstructions in the chimney. I'll need a fire built for the tea kettle and to heat water for cleaning."

Mr. Craig took a knee in front of the hearth. "I'll tend to the fireplaces."

"Mr. Gibbons, there are several buckets at the back door. If you would fill them with water, please? There's a well and pump out back."

Mr. Gibbons nodded. "Yes, ma'am."

They worked together for several hours. The men made multiple trips to the wagon hauling old flour sacks, rusted tins, and the tattered curtains, rugs, and mattress they dragged down from the apartment. The uncovering of the fine red tile floor in the workroom made a welcome bonus.

Anne would enlist the carpenter to salvage the two broken chairs laying in a corner in the front room. She would sew cushions for them, and they would fit perfectly beside one of the front windows for her customers to sit and chat.

When they had removed the table from the back room and placed it in front of the large display window, Anne leaned against it. "This is where I'll do most of my work. The windows will provide a good source of light."

"Hello," Amelia called out from the entrance. "Iris says it's time to break for lunch." She stepped inside and stopped at the sight of the men. "I wasn't aware you had company."

"This is Mr. Craig and Mr. Gibbons. Gentlemen, this is a friend, Amelia Stanford. They are employees of Michael's. He sent them. And I must say, they have been quite wonderful. I don't know what I would have done without them." Anne took the basket from Amelia, who curtsied to the gentlemen.

Mr. Gibbons had not taken his eyes off Amelia. "It's our pleasure," he said, bowing and shuffling his feet.

"Is there enough food to share with—" Anne began.

A huge russet-brown hound dog bounded through the doorway and circled around Anne's feet, almost knocking her over.

"Not to fret, miss." Mr. Gibbons signaled for the dog to sit.

"This is Bramble, Mr. Harrigan's dog. Where the dog is, Miss Cate is never far behind."

As if on cue, a young girl around ten years old ran inside and joined the group circled around Bramble. Her clothing mimicked that of the men—canvas breeches, red-and-black-checked shirt, and boots. Though she dressed in male attire, she was one of the loveliest creatures Anne had ever encountered. Her flawless creamy complexion, her ebony hair she wore in a waist-length plait, and her moss-green eyes made for a stunning visage. Had her mother been this beautiful? It was no wonder Michael continued to grieve. Self-conscious, Anne straightened her mobcap.

"Naughty dog, are you being rude again?" Cate admonished the dog.

Bramble looked up at her adoringly, not the least bit chastened.

Michael strode through the doorway, filling the room with his presence. His dark-green waistcoat accentuated his hazel eyes and fitted his physique to a tee. Anne studied his form—wide shoulders, broad chest, narrow waist, long, muscular limbs. A tailor's dream. A woman's dream.

She was staring. Had he noticed? Her cheeks grew hot.

"Good morning, Anne...Amelia." His expression remained impassive. "Cate, did you and Bramble barge in without formal introductions?" His smile tempered any reprimand.

Cate ducked her head for a moment, and then she made a gracious curtsy that would have impressed the king's court. "I do beg your pardon, ladies. I am Caitlin Harrigan and this is Bramble. We are most pleased to make your acquaintance."

Watching his daughter's performance, Michael's eyes danced. He scanned the room and the newly polished floors. "Looks as if the cleanup is going well." He stepped closer to Anne and brushed a smudge from her cheek with his thumb.

Why, oh why, was it that every time she encountered him, she was disheveled and covered in some sort of grime or other?

Amelia clasped her hands together in front of her all prim and proper, dressed in a frilly china-blue dress. Not one tendril of her hair had gone astray.

"Thanks to Mr. Craig and Mr. Gibbons"—Anne nodded to the men—"we are progressing nicely. I can't thank you enough, Michael, for sending them to help me. They aren't needed at your mill? I wouldn't want to put you out."

"Not to worry. We won't get busy until next month with the new cutting season." He patted Bramble, who had pressed against his leg. "Fellows, looks as if you have a wagonload. Why don't you haul it away and give Miss Forbes a chance to rest a few minutes and enjoy her repast?"

Anne followed them to the door. "Thank you, gentlemen. I appreciate what you've done. Once I'm ready for business, I insist you stop by and I'll make you checked shirts. I saw bolts of the material in the mercantile."

The men shared a glance and then directed their attention to Michael, who shook his head.

"There's no need, Miss Forbes. We don't need payment," Mr. Craig said.

She grinned. "Oh, but I have a selfish motive. Once the other lumbermen see my work, they will want shirts of their own."

Mr. Craig looked again to his employer. Michael nodded his approval this time. "That's a fine idea. We'll be back when you're open for business. It might be time for me to get a new waistcoat as well for Sunday services. We'll bid you good day."

Mr. Gibbons grabbed the damaged chairs on his way out. "We'll drop these off at the carpenter's."

Anne handed the basket back to Amelia and untied and unpinned her apron. "I'm famished."

Amelia opened the basket top. "There's plenty to share, Michael, if you and Cate would like to join us."

Michael put his hand on Cate's shoulder. "I'd like nothing more, but I have business in town."

"But, Papa." Cate focused her lovely eyes on him. "May I stay, please?"

Michael locked eyes with Anne, and she almost lost her breath. What a disturbingly handsome man.

"Of...of course. Cate is most welcome." She had stuttered.

Why was she acting such a clod? They had spent weeks together on the trail. She knew him, his movements, expressions, and mannerisms almost as well as she knew her brother's and father's. But he was not either of them. Not a relative. Not a friend, but the man who had captured her heart.

"If Anne is agreeable, then I'll come back in a couple of hours for you, Kitten." He motioned to Bramble as the dog stood and made a long stretch. "You stay with Cate, boy."

The adoration for his daughter softened Michael's features. What would it be like to be cherished by him? For him to look at her that way? Could she even dream of such a thing?

"Ladies." He bowed his head and left the shop, taking a good bit of the air with him.

The dog flopped back down. Anne enjoyed the hound's antics. Should she look into getting her own dog? For company...for protection? Protection from what? The community felt as safe as any place she had ever resided.

"Bramble is such an unusual name. How did he come by it?" Anne ruffled the dog's ears.

Cate giggled. "I gave it to him. When he was born, his mama hid him and two other puppies among some bramble bushes. You see, a wolf had been lurking around." She dropped to her knees and wrapped her arms around the dog's neck. "The mama and the two brothers climbed out of the bush, but he got stuck. I had to crawl among the thorns to get him out. And so, the name Bramble."

What an enchanting young lady. Even in such short acquaintance, she had already wound herself around Anne's heart.

Anne grimaced at her filthy arms and hands. "I need to get clean before I eat."

In the back, she washed in one of the buckets and then joined Amelia and Cate at the work table.

Amelia glanced around the room. "We have no chairs."

"We'll sit up here." Anne hopped onto the edge of the table. "Did you know that tailors in shops back home sit atop tables like this to do their work? That way, they take full advantage of the light from the window."

"If so, it's very awkward," said Amelia as she twisted this way and that trying to find the best way to climb onto the table.

Cate gave her a leg up and grinned at Anne before springing up beside her.

What a darling girl. And such an impish smile.

Anne had not realized how truly hungry she was until she bit into one of the scones. They had not long finished eating when the two men who worked for Iris entered the shop carrying Anne's trunk of tailoring supplies.

"Perfect timing, gentlemen. Put it here, if you please." Anne pointed to a spot beside the work table.

The men did as she bade, tipped their hats, and left.

With Cate standing close by, Anne opened the chest and clapped her hands. "All is intact."

The smells that wafted from inside—cedar, the sweet scent of lavender from the bits she placed inside, and the familiar aroma of woven materials—evoked a sudden yearning for home. Caught off guard, Anne sucked in a breath.

Cate touched her elbow. "Is something amiss?"

Deep compassion shone in the young girl's eyes. She was her father's daughter, even mimicking his turn of phrase.

"I'm fine. I was reminded of my home...my family...for a moment."

Amelia remained a while sweeping away the few remaining spider webs. "Uh-uh. That's enough for me," she said, leaning the broom against the work table. "If I continue, I'll be filthy." She smiled at Cate. "It was lovely meeting you. I hope to see you again." She swung the lunch basket onto her arm. "I'll see you at Iris's, Anne? You mustn't overwork yourself."

"I'll be there for supper."

Anne stood at the entrance and watched Amelia walk away toward the boarding house. Their newfound friendship warmed her heart. It had started with Amelia's illness and Anne's fervent prayers for her recovery. Anne had admired the young woman's bravery when faced with the fear of disfigurement. With the death of her best friend, she had endured a tragic ordeal and had come through the other side changed, more serious and less selfish. Their relationship grew even more pleasant when Amelia ended her outrageous flirting with Michael, though she did sometimes hold on to him more than Anne preferred.

Cate held up two male dolls she had taken from the chest. "Look at these," she said with delight.

One was dressed in everyday clothes of brown waistcoat, white shirt and cravat, tan breeches and stockings. The other wore a silver-embroidered dark-blue coat, matching vest, and breeches. Blue satin bows festooned the tops of his stockings.

"They are my models. Samples of work I can do."

Cate studied the formally attired doll and ran her fingers down the coat seams. "You made these clothes? The stitches are so tiny. I have never touched such beautiful material. You amaze me."

"You are too kind." Anne took the mannequins that were

the length of her forearm. "Let's put them in the display window."

Cate peered into the trunk. "You have female models?"

"Not yet. I had hoped to purchase them before leaving Scotland but didn't have the time."

Outside, two women walking down the street stopped at the window to gape at the dolls. Their expressions of amazement mirrored Cate's.

Anne pulled bolts of cloth from the trunk, brown and white linens and wools for men's breeches, a length of precious white cotton for the best quality shirts and cravats, dark-brown and green lightweight wool for frockcoats and jackets, and low-grade linens for men's market wallets. As she arranged them on shelves next to the work table, her hands itched to begin her work.

Cate felt the corner of a bolt of blue satin. "This feels lovely."

"Yes, and it's costly. Tailors don't ordinarily sell fabric. But I wasn't certain what I would find in the colonies. I've made arrangements with the proprietor of the mercantile about helping my customers order their preferences."

"There's a lot to this tailoring. How did you learn?"

Anne examined a length of Irish lace intended for a wedding dress. For her own wedding someday? "I apprenticed with a tailor back home in Scotland."

Cate cocked her head. "When did you know that it was what you wanted to do?"

"I was about eight."

"Eight! I am nine and have no idea what I wish to do with my life."

Anne patted her cheek. "You have plenty of time to think about it, Cate."

Anne gathered a half-dozen white linen mobcaps and placed them on the work table. She would decide later where to display them. Finally, she had emptied the trunk, and all the cloth, tools, and notions claimed their proper places.

Anne clicked shut the lock of the chest. "That's that."

She put a basket of ribbons and brightly dyed silk scarves on a small, three-legged table next to one of the front windows. Cate shuffled through the ribbons, pulled one from the basket, and ran it through her fingers.

"It matches your eyes." Anne tied it in a bow at the end of Cate's braid. "My gift for helping me."

Cate's eyes grew soft, and suddenly, she clasped Anne in a fervent hug. Her head reached just below Anne's chin, and Anne could not resist kissing the top of it.

"You are the kindest lady. I cannot wait to show it to Papa."

Anne held up the list she had been compiling and dropped it into her woven grass shopping basket. "Let's you and I visit the mercantile."

"I should like that." Cate twirled around. "May we have tea? There's a garden at the back where Mrs. Hale serves scrumptious scones. Not as good as Mrs. Iris's but good."

How did one refuse those entreating green eyes?

Anne threw her apron onto the work table. "Mm.... I would adore a cup of tea."

They walked outside and Bramble followed. "Will he accompany us?"

Cate patted the dog's head. "Bramble is welcome everywhere I go."

Anne searched her under-pocket for a key and locked the doors. What a glorious feeling to be locking the door to her own shop.

As they walked the short distance to the mercantile, passersby greeted Cate, who gaily nodded or waved. Some acknowledged Anne. Though she did not know them yet, they knew her. They welcomed her. She belonged—a feeling that warmed her to her core.

Inside the store, Anne purchased lengths of red-and-black-checked wool as well as enough yellow checked gauze for bedroom curtains. She bought two blue hooked rugs—the larger for the side of her bed and a smaller one for underneath her rocking chair she planned to place between her fireplace and the window. Her last acquisition was a downy-filled mattress. Before going out the back door to the tea room, she made arrangements with the proprietor to deliver her purchases.

Outside, she and Cate sat at one of three tables beside a huge oak tree with branches that formed a canopy overhead. Clay pots bursting with azaleas, lilies, and daisies lined a stone-walled courtyard.

"Thank you for bringing me here, Cate. It's the stuff dreams are made of. I expect to catch a fairy peeping out from behind one of the flowerpots."

Cate giggled. "I knew you would like it." She straightened up in her chair. "You are not to worry about my manners. Mrs. Iris and Cookie have spent hours teaching me things such as the proper way to drink tea. I shall be a lady one day and will want to make Papa proud."

"Cookie?"

"He's the old gentleman who cooks for us and for Papa's workers. When I say old, I mean he looks to be a hundred."

Anne snickered.

"Because of him, I know how to make pancakes and apple pies." She opened her napkin and spread it across her lap. "But the thing I like most is wandering the woods with Bramble. I adore climbing trees. There's a particular one I've had my eye on, a giant black willow that's growing beside a waterfall a good distance from our house. It's a bit frightening, but I plan to conquer it one day." She leaned forward. "Papa would have an apoplexy if he knew. So...promise you will keep it a secret?"

"I don't know. It sounds a bit dangerous. Maybe—"

Mrs. Hale, the proprietress, approached the table carrying a teapot. "You are Anne Forbes?" she asked as she filled their cups with steaming tea.

"I am."

"You spoke with Mr. Hale on your previous visit. I'm sorry I missed you, but I'm happy to make your acquaintance now. We've been in want of a tailor and seamstress." She placed a plate of blueberry scones on the table. "When you are ready to open your shop, I'd like to speak to you about sewing some dresses for me."

"I look forward to it, Mrs. Hale."

What a delightful, encouraging start to her business.

"Enjoy the scones. The blueberries are fresh. I picked them off the bushes over there in the corner of the garden." She motioned to Bramble as he curled next to Cate's feet. "Here's something for you, too, boy." She threw a biscuit to the dog. He caught it and devoured it in seconds, then settled back down and promptly fell asleep.

Cate put a half-eaten scone on her plate and sipped her tea. "This is so good. I'm glad Papa and Uncle Cal aren't here."

Anne raised her eyebrow at the peculiar remark. "Why is that?"

Cate chewed a bit of scone, swallowed, and then beamed. "They both have a terrible sweet tooth. When they were boys, they fought over cookies, pies, syrup for their pancakes... anything sweet. Uncle Cal says that, despite Papa being nine years older, he often lost those fights." She brushed some crumbs from her shirt. "I suspect that Papa let him win. He's like that, you know."

A picture of the two handsome, ebony-haired boys craving and fighting over sweets made Anne smile. She concurred with Cate's observation that Michael probably let his younger brother win, and agreed that he was like that. She treasured the tidbit of information about Michael. She made a fairly good apple pie. Maybe she would make one just for him.

After Anne and Cate finished their tea, they returned to Anne's shop to find her purchases stacked outside next to the entrance.

To her delight, Michael walked up behind them. Without a word, he threw the mattress over his shoulder and headed upstairs. Anne followed and watched him arrange the mattress on the rope springs and sit on the edge.

He bounced a couple of times. "This will be comfortable."

Anne had imagined Michael on her bed a number of times. Her face grew hot. To see him there made her gulp.

"Will you be comfortable here?" He glanced around. "I don't mean only in this room, but in Graniteville?"

"I believe I will. It's a lovely town, and so far, I've met people I feel will be good friends one day."

She would be content in any place where Michael resided.

"That pleases me." He motioned to the door. "Shall we?"

Cate waited for them at the bottom of the steps. "Come see the dolls, Papa." She grabbed his hand and tugged him to the mannequins.

Michael regarded the dolls, his eyebrows arched. "Impressive."

He draped Cate's plait over her shoulder and touched the bow in her hair. "A new ribbon?"

Cate beamed. "Miss Anne gave it to me."

He playfully tapped her nose. "It matches your eyes."

The deep love between father and daughter ignited a yearning within Anne so profound, her entire body ached.

"But we must go, Kitten. Let's give Miss Anne a respite. Yes?"

Cate ducked her head. "Yes. Thank you, Miss Anne, for a lovely day. I look forward to seeing you again."

"That may be sooner than you imagine." Michael stood behind Cate and rested his hands on her shoulders. "My brother, Cal, and I would love for you to come to dinner day after tomorrow. It's early times for Cal's bereavement, but he wants to thank you for caring for Megan."

The terrible memory of the woman's suffering and tragic death scored Anne's heart. Grief for Keith hurt as much as the day he passed. Had it been only a few weeks?

Michael studied her face. "I asked Amelia and Iris on my way here. They accepted. What say you?"

"I would love to."

Anne's pulse raced. How exciting—an opportunity not only to meet Cal but to see where Michael lived.

CHAPTER 16

*T*he following day, after Anne and Iris finished their afternoon tea, Anne leaned her elbows on the table and folded her hands under her chin.

"If I may ask, Iris, there is something I need your help with."

"I'm listening."

"I will need assistance in the shop. A young person...maybe two. One must be a male to take the measurements of my gentlemen customers. I would teach them the trade, of course, and give them a small recompense."

"I know the very young people." Iris scooted back her chair. "I could introduce you to them now, if you are amenable. They live in Grace Holler a couple of miles from here."

"Holler?"

"Ha! I imagine the word does sound strange to you. A holler is a cut-out place on the side of a mountain." Her brows knitted. "Think of it as a piece of pie. All the way up each side of the cut-out, people build cabins with pathways in between."

"I'm not sure I can picture it."

Iris laughed. "You have to see it. Come. I shall enjoy showing it to you."

After leaving the boarding house, they walked through the town and circled behind the church. There they took a narrow road that cut through a forest and then became a path that gradually wound up a steep incline.

"My ears are popping." Anne pressed her hands to her ears. "My knees burn a little too."

Iris grinned at Anne over her shoulder. "Tug a bit on your earlobes and open your mouth wide. You'll get used to the feeling. It occurs the higher up you go. Though this isn't one of the highest mountains around here."

A huge tree in the distance caught Anne's attention, and she stopped and pointed. "What is that? It looks like a tree, but there's a door and...a window...carved in the trunk!"

Three children, all clearly in need of a good meal, lingered in front of the giant oak, so big it would take fifty paces to walk around it.

"It's a tree house. A family lives inside it." Iris's blue eyes sparkled.

Anne would not have been more surprised if Iris had grown wheat stalks out of her mobcap. "You are joshing."

"It is rather astonishing the first time one sees it."

To Anne's amazement, the door in the tree trunk opened, a woman walked out of it and stood behind her children. All were dressed in drab, worn clothing that blended with the gray tree bark.

"Our pastor is the only person who's ever been allowed inside. I understand the tree is hollow halfway up with places for eating and sleeping. It even accommodates a stove."

Anne tucked in her chin and blinked.

"The family living inside is too poor to afford a house, but they have refused all offers of assistance. They've been there about five years now."

"I cannot find words." Anne shook her head. "If I hadn't seen it with my own eyes, I don't think I would have believed you."

Iris laughed and waved to the children, but none of them returned her greeting. "Let's continue on. They don't take to intruders."

They broke through the forest to the sight of a gap in the side of a mountain with log cabins situated on levels from the bottom to the top on either side of the crevice.

"The Camerons live there." Iris pointed to the second level of dwellings.

They followed a path to a cabin the exterior of which had faded into light gray battered from generations of severe weather. On the front porch, a woman pumped a wooden stick up and down into a barrel.

When she spotted Anne and Iris, she walked down the two steps of the porch and approached them, wiping her hands on her apron. "Mrs. Clarendon, good day to ye."

The short, stout woman folded her arms across her stomach. Her smile lit up her bright green eyes. Coils of rust-red hair curled out from under her pristine mobcap and framed her plump face. Wrinkles creased the sides of her eyes to her temples. This person laughed a lot.

"A good day to you, Mrs. Cameron." Iris motioned toward Anne. "May I introduce my friend Anne Forbes? She has opened a tailor shop in our town."

Anne returned the woman's curtsy. "A pleasure."

"Won't you sit a while?" Mrs. Cameron led them up the stairs where they sat on rustic wooden chairs.

Anne scanned the other side of the holler and the small homes nestled among oak, pine, and hickory nut trees. "You have a fine prospect here, Mrs. Cameron. I hope we aren't interrupting your work?"

"Not at all. I'm makin' butter. It can wait." She crossed her ankles and ran her fingers along the creases in her petticoats. "How may I help you?"

"As I mentioned, Miss Forbes has opened a tailor shop. She would like to hire two young people to assist her. She plans to teach them the trade. I thought Christopher and Katherine would suit the job well."

Mrs. Cameron's face registered surprise and then delight. "Aye. That's a fine idea. Let me go inside and fetch them. This is their readin' time."

She came back in a couple of minutes accompanied by a girl and boy of about fourteen. Mirror images of each other, they had their mother's green eyes and thick russet hair.

"Miss Forbes, these are my twins, Katherine and Christopher."

"I'm pleased to meet you," said Anne.

The twins favored each other down to the pattern of freckles spattered across their noses and on their cheeks.

"Children, Miss Forbes is looking to hire apprentices."

The young people shared a glance, and both smiled broadly.

Anne held out her hands. "I would teach you how to be a tailor and give you a small salary. You would be required to work twelve hours a day, from seven to seven. Six days a week. Those are my same hours."

"I'd be more than pleased, Miss Forbes." Christopher curled his fingers around his sister's hand. "Katherine agrees... don't you?"

"Mighty pleased," Katherine answered.

"We'd have to get my husband's permission. He ain't home right now. He works at the sawmill." Mrs. Cameron slid her hands into her apron pockets.

"Of course." Anne stood next to the twins, who were almost as tall as she. "If their father is amenable, I'd want them to start in two days. Would that suit?"

Mrs. Cameron nodded.

"As for clothing…" Anne perused Katherine's brown bodice, striped petticoats, and mobcap as well as Christopher's trade shirt, canvas breeches, and stockings. Both were clean and tidy, and they both wore latchet shoes. "What you are wearing will do nicely. Eventually, we will make you uniforms. That will be our first project together. Yes?"

The twins beamed, and their friendly eyes twinkled.

Satisfied, Anne and Iris bade their farewells.

Her spirits light, Anne matched her footsteps to Iris's as they descended the holler. "I have a good feeling about those two."

"Yes, 'tis a good decision."

As they passed by the tree house family, Anne made a mental note to find ways to help them. After all, if she left parcels of food without letting them see her, they could not turn them down. She considered her decision to hire the twins and was pleased with herself. Would Michael agree? The opportunity to ask him would present itself tomorrow when they dined together.

CHAPTER 17

*A*nne practically danced from one foot to the other in the back garden of the boarding house waiting with Amelia and Iris for their ride to supper.

When Michael appeared on horseback preceding a phaeton driven by a man who could have been his twin, she pressed her hand down the folds in her petticoats and checked the ribbon of her straw hat tied at the back of her neck. Heeding Amelia's criticism of her perpetual wearing of brown, she wore pale-pink petticoats with a dark-rose overskirt and bodice.

Michael dismounted next to her, and the glint of admiration in his eyes more than compensated for the extra care she had taken with her toilette.

He leaned down. "Good evening, Anne. You look lovely."

Before she could think of a response, Cal, favoring his leg, climbed down from the buggy and made a bow. "You must be Miss Forbes. I've heard a great many things about you."

Anne curtsied to the gentleman. His features mirrored Michael's—dark hair, hazel eyes, full beard. Cal favored his brother physically, but his pleasant, open demeanor set him apart from his more sober sibling.

"I hope they were complimentary things. And, please, call me Anne."

"They couldn't be more complimentary. Michael told me you cared for my wife until she passed." He glanced away for a moment. "This evening is a way for me to thank you. I'm in your debt, Anne"

She studied his eyes, so like Michael's. They reflected much pain in their depths. "Please accept my deepest condolences, Mr. Harrigan. And there is no debt. All of the wagoners pitched in. We did what was necessary."

"You are too humble, Anne. And I'd be honored if you'd call me Cal."

"I should like that."

What an agreeable man. Almost as appealing as his brother.

Cal bowed to Iris. "Mrs. Iris, you look handsome this evening."

Iris tapped Cal's forearm. "I would add my condolences. Megan was a lovely woman."

"Thank you, dear lady. She thought well of you. As do I." He turned to Amelia. "I'm happy to see you again. It's been a long time. You look as stunning as ever." He held her hand. "I hope you are recovering from our mutual loss."

Amelia looked down at their hands, and her bottom lip trembled. "I miss Megan. And some other time, may we speak of her? Share our grief?"

Cal patted her hand before releasing it. "We'll make plans."

Michael clasped Anne's elbow. "Ladies, let's get you settled. Anne and Iris, if you would...sit in the back seat. Amelia will sit up front with Cal." He helped Anne onto the seat and then assisted Iris. "We're only ten miles away, so it will be a short ride. The road is fairly smooth."

He mounted his horse and waited for Amelia and Cal to be seated. With Michael at the lead, Cal swiftly maneuvered their carriage out of town and onto a road that meandered through a valley between fields of corn and tobacco.

Cal snapped the reins. "Have you had an opportunity to walk any of our mountain trails, Amelia?"

Amelia gave him a sideways glance. "Not yet."

Iris ducked her head down to whisper in Anne's ear. "For someone who prizes her creature comforts as much as Amelia, hiking the mountains seems a most unlikely occurrence. Don't you agree?"

Anne could not stifle her giggle.

Michael slowed his horse next to her and motioned toward a field of vines supported by stakes and twine. "Look, Anne. Over there, someone is experimenting with growing grapes. They haven't had much luck with the vines they brought from Italy, but this area has the correct weather and soil. Our little community may eventually have a vineyard to boast of."

Iris poked Anne with her elbow. "Michael takes pride in our little settlement."

"I know. He could talk of nothing else on our way here. From what I've experienced so far, he has a right to be proud."

They soon entered a forest thick with pines, oaks, and countless other trees. The underbrush teamed with lush mountain laurels, seedling cedars, and rhododendron bushes. The sights, sounds, and smells brought Anne's senses alive.

"Look at the wildflowers...and all those black-eyed Susans." Anne pointed to a meadow they were passing. "There are so many colors. God has put on a show for us. It takes my breath away."

A thundering sound of water echoed through the woods.

"Is that a waterfall, Michael?" Anne asked.

He twisted around in the saddle. "It is."

"Could you take me there one day?"

"It would be my pleasure. We'll make a day of it and take Cate. It's one of her favorite spots to swim. I know you don't swim. We'll have to fix that."

Anne cocked her head.

"You told me once." He winked.

Ah, yes, the skunk. She smiled back.

They entered a valley where Anne caught sight of the brothers' house. An L-shaped porch wrapped around the two-story log structure nestled against a mountain with row upon row of cedar trees climbing up to the sky. The porch faced a grass-covered valley and a mountain with a bald spot near the top.

Anne motioned toward it. "What happened on that mountain?"

Cal halted the carriage at the front steps of the house. "Fire. It's one of our gravest fears. They are mostly caused by lightning." He hopped down and held his arm out for Amelia. "We've tried to create breaks in the forest...places where we level areas and clear them of debris."

Michael assisted Iris and then Anne. His fingers curled around hers as they stood next to the carriage. Contact with him stirred her, and she did not want to let go.

Amelia moved in a half circle taking in the house and grounds. "This is stunning. Megan's descriptions may have misled me."

Sadness dulled Cal's eyes. "She would have preferred living in Philadelphia."

Amelia touched Cal's forearm. "Megan was a social person. She enjoyed parties, music, and lively conversations. She was a dear friend, and I miss her terribly. Grief for her is something we have in common. I repeat my offer should you ever want to share with me."

This new, more compassionate side to Amelia deepened Anne's affection for her.

"Hello, everyone," Cate called from the front door. "I'm happy you've come for a visit. I know we'll have a grand time."

Anne had seen Cate at church in the dress she now wore. The moss-green striped bodice and petticoats, the same color as her eyes, accentuated her flawless complexion and coal-black hair. Was it possible for the girl to be any prettier? Her eyes sparkled as she descended the stairs.

"You look lovely," Anne said, taking in the ruffles across the bodice. A fine seamstress had fashioned Cate's ensemble.

Suddenly, Anne pictured a line of suitors climbing up the front steps. Michael was going to have his hands full when his daughter came of age. But beauty was not Cate's only attribute. God had granted her a keen mind, an inquisitive nature, and a sweet, kind disposition. Anne hoped she would be present to meet the man who eventually won Cate's hand and made it past her father's scrutiny.

Cate patted the ribbon in her hair. "It's the one you gave me."

The gesture pleased Anne. "I see."

A gentleman with gray hair and a full gray beard and who stood over six feet tall strode out the front door and across the porch. He wore a white linen apron pinned to his shirt, and he brandished a wooden spoon. "Dinner will be served in a few minutes."

"Thank you, Cookie. We look forward to it." Michael nodded toward the older man. "Ladies, this is our chef. He not only cooks the family's meals, but sees to it that our workers are fed three times a day. That includes a breakfast of two- to three-hundred pancakes for our forty-man camp and a day's baking that might include ten pies or twenty loaves of bread."

Anne curtsied. "That's astonishing, Cookie. You have my sincere admiration. Cate mentioned that you have taught her how to bake pies and pancakes."

Cookie grinned. "Much appreciated, Miss Forbes. Cate

speaks of you often. I hope to visit your shop one day. I'm in need of a new waistcoat."

"Maybe we could barter. A waistcoat for your pies?"

"I look forward to making that trade." Cookie saluted her with his spoon and went back inside.

"It's ironic that someone so"—Anne searched for the word —"imposing...should have such a sweet name as *Cookie*."

Michael chortled. "Sweet? As you can imagine, no one has ever challenged him about it."

"I can understand."

"May I show you the house?" Michael held out his arms for Anne and Iris, and they ascended the steps and passed through the front entrance.

Cal escorted Amelia and Cate, who giggled at her uncle's formality.

The inside of the house with its polished heart-pine floors and huge fireplace impressed Anne almost as much as the exterior. A burl oak cabinet with its distinctive mottled pattern and brass drawer handles rested in a corner on a dark-blue hook rug. A dining table that seated eight dominated the center of the room. Two pewter candelabras decorated with greenery sat in the middle of the table with white candles waiting to be lit. On one side of the room, a teakwood occasional table nestled between two tapestry chairs. A partially finished chess game lay on the table. Shades of blue and yellow—curtains, chair cushions, rugs, and table coverings—offset the dark floors and furniture.

Amelia pointed to a hutch at the side of the room. "What beautiful porcelain pieces."

"They were our mother's. Brought over from England." Cal motioned to the hutch. "Would you care to see them?"

While the two of them viewed the porcelain collection, Anne joined Iris and Cate in front of the fireplace. Michael lingered by the door.

Anne motioned toward the painting that hung above the mantel. "This must be your mother."

"It is." Cate's brow furrowed. "I never had the chance to know her."

Anne studied the portrait. A skilled artist had captured the grace and elegance of the stunning woman poised in a field of wildflowers. Anne's pink dress paled in comparison to the moss-green satin gown that matched Heather's eyes. How could a woman compete with such perfection? Her heart felt heavy.

"Cate," Cal called out. "Would you join us? Amelia has a question about one of these pieces."

"Excuse me." Cate, who had been watching Anne's face, moved next to her uncle.

"Heather was a beautiful woman," said Iris. "Cate favors her. She was clever and kind and sensitive to other people's needs. This room still feels like her—warm, inviting, welcoming. She and Michael were favorites of our society—what there is of it."

No wonder Michael had never remarried.

"She died giving birth to Cate, you know," Iris said in a lowered voice.

"I didn't know for certain. I wondered, but I didn't want to pry." Anne perused the room. "This is a huge house."

"Yes. I've visited many times, and I am impressed each time. There are two master bedrooms, Cate's room, and two other bedrooms. There's a fine kitchen behind the house. If asked, I'm certain Cookie would be proud to show it to you."

"I don't know. He seems intimidating. I wouldn't wish to disturb his domain."

"Michael, Heather, and Cal added onto the original house. Designed it as a compound of sorts in hopes of sharing it with their families." Iris watched Cal conversing with Amelia. "Poor Cal. To have lost his wife so soon. They were married only two years when Megan left for Scotland to settle her aunt's affairs.

Between the trip over and the trip back, she was away almost a year. She never liked it here, though." Iris sniffed. "But I gossip. Forgive me."

Michael walked to the center of the room. "Everyone, why don't we sit on the porch and give Cookie time to set the table? Most importantly, there's a promise of a beautiful sunset this evening."

They all filed out of the house to sit in the chairs lined across the porch.

Cate motioned to Anne. "Come sit by me."

Anne happily obliged. Michael sat on her other side. Everyone remained quiet watching the cerulean sky slowly turn pink, then magenta and purple.

Drawn to the splendid sight, Anne stood and leaned against the porch rail.

Cate pressed against her side and twined her fingers through Anne's. "It is beautiful, isn't it?" she whispered.

"It's magnificent."

Michael moved beside her, pressing his hands on the railing.

Suddenly, a brilliant yellow-orange ray shot through the purple clouds and lit the tops of the cedar trees on the mountain across the valley.

Anne sucked in a deep breath. "They look as if they are on fire." She squeezed Cate's fingers. "Our Lord is sharing His wondrous creation with us. I could stand here forever."

"I think I like that idea," Michael murmured.

Had she heard him correctly? What was his meaning? Hope, similar to the shaft of sunlight they had just witnessed, lit inside Anne's heart.

Cookie, who had waited in the doorway enjoying the sunset with them, announced, "Dinner is served, Mr. Harrigan."

Anne fairly floated to the dining table. Her spirits remained high throughout dinner. She barely registered what was served, and twice, Cate had to repeat a remark she made Anne's way. When they finished their meal, she added her congratulations to Cookie, who beamed with pride.

Michael pushed back from the table and stood. "Shall we all go for a stroll?"

Cal rubbed his midriff. "Brilliant idea. I need to walk. Cookie outdid himself, and I confess, I indulged more than I should." He held his arm out to Amelia. "Shall we?"

Iris sighed. "You young people go ahead. I'm laying claim to one of those porch rockers."

Although the night had not completely taken over the day, Michael lit a lantern, and with Anne and Cate on either side, he led the way toward the stream that meandered behind the house and through the valley.

They neared a row of mountain laurel bushes when Amelia stumbled on a root and clasped Cal's arm. "My ankle."

Cal put one arm around her waist and held her hand with the other. "Can you walk?"

She tried pressing her foot on the ground but faltered. "No. It's quite painful."

"If I may?" Cal swept Amelia into his arms and strode across the yard, up the stairs, and inside the house.

The rest of them quickly followed and waited while Cal settled Amelia onto one of the upholstered chairs.

Iris followed them inside and rested her hand on Amelia's shoulder. "Whatever happened?"

"She tripped." Cal knelt in front of Amelia, who trembled and fought back tears. "May I examine your ankle?"

Amelia nodded.

He lifted her petticoats and removed her shoe. Very tenderly, he prodded her ankle bones. "Nothing's broken. But it is beginning to swell a bit."

"I'll get some ice," Michael offered.

"You have ice?" Anne exclaimed.

"We do. Would you like to see?"

"I would."

Outside, Michael picked up a lantern and led the way to a small shed that had been built over the stream. He opened the door and lifted the lantern, lighting a block of ice packed in straw.

Anne gasped.

"We bring the ice down from the highest mountains and store it here. The stream water stays frigid year round and keeps it from melting." He took out his knife, chopped off a sliver, and handed it to her.

Anne put the shard to her lips and sucked on it. Freezing water dribbled down her chin. "Oh my! I've never experienced such a thing. It's quite exhilarating."

Michael wiped her chin with his thumb. Locking eyes with hers, he leaned down and covered her lips with his.

Overwhelming sensations—hot shafts and icy shards—took turns shooting through her body, tingling in the pit of her stomach. He did not embrace her. Their only contact was the soft, warm feel of his lips caressing hers.

He slowly released her lips and drew back. "I can't tell you how I have longed to do that."

Breathless, Anne could not form an answer.

"Did it please you, Anne?"

"Aye, Michael. Very much."

"Papa," Cate shouted from the porch. "We need the ice."

He glanced over his shoulder and sighed. "We will speak more...later. I feel we have much to talk about."

Would that conversation change her life?

CHAPTER 18

*a*fter a restless night, Michael rode out from his house before dawn the next morning. The feel of Anne's mouth beneath his...her breath against his lips...and her trembling body had kept him awake most of the night. He prided himself on his self-control, but with Anne, he had lost it. He could not resist putting into action the dreams of kissing her that had preoccupied him.

Not far from the house, he stopped at the family cemetery and walked straight to Heather's gravesite. He ran his fingers across the top of the granite headstone with its engraving— *Beloved Wife and Mother...A Daughter of the King.* A woman of deep faith, she had felt joy calling herself by that name.

"Dear one," he whispered. "I have met someone. Someone I love deeply and want to spend the rest of my life with. You would adore Anne. I believe our Cate loves her as well, and that Anne will make a wonderful mother to our daughter. I miss you, Heather, but I must move on. It's time."

The painful bubble of sorrow he had carried inside him nine years suddenly burst, freeing him to fill his lungs with fresh, renewing air.

Before leaving the cemetery, he paused at the graves where his parents were laid to rest. His mother would have given him sound advice, but only when asked. She would have accompanied it with a hefty piece of her famous apple pie and a glass of milk. Sober, staunch Presbyterians, she and Michael's father had passed eight years previously from influenza. He remembered them often with abounding love and respect.

He mounted his horse and headed for the mountain that bordered his land. Halfway up, when the trail became too hazardous to ride, he tethered the horse.

When he patted the mare's neck, she whickered. "I won't be long, girl."

Taking a well-worn path, he reached the pinnacle. Sweaty and out of breath, he removed his tricorn, dropped to his knees, and prayed. He had so many questions. Was he making a wise decision? He felt a bond between them, but did Anne feel as strongly about him as he did her? If he asked her to marry him, what if she refused? It did not bear considering. Most important of all, would it please the Lord? He asked for wisdom to make the right decision and offered thanksgiving for his many blessings.

He walked to the precipice just as the sun peeked over the rolling blue-hazed mountains in the distance. Michael was not one to believe in signs, but the awesome rays splashing gold across the sky refreshed his spirits. He would ask Anne to be his wife. If she said *no*, he would make it his life's purpose to change her mind.

As he descended the mountain, questions about how he would go about winning over Anne beset his mind. He would seek Cal's advice. Eager for answers, he rode past their home and through the forest to the sawmill where he found his brother sitting behind the desk in the office.

"You left out early." Cal rocked back in his chair.

Michael straddled a chair and leaned his arms across its back brace. "I had a lot on my mind."

"Such as?"

"I want to ask Anne to marry me."

"Well, now, that *is* a lot to have on your mind." Cal righted his chair. "Though I'm not surprised."

Michael raised an eyebrow.

"Anyone with half-decent eyesight can see that you're besotted with her."

"I..." Michael hesitated. "Is it that obvious?"

"It is. And I couldn't be happier for you. Anne is a lovely person. A perfect foil for you."

Michael blinked. "What?"

"Where you are sober, she is lighthearted. Where you keep your feelings close to your chest, she is an open book. Where she is talented, sensitive, and creative, you own a boring sawmill."

"You're making fun, right?"

Cal chuckled. "I am, brother. I couldn't help myself. You're looking so pitifully lovelorn, I had to do something."

"Seriously, Cal, I need help. Anne and I began our relationship as friends, but my feelings have grown much deeper, and I sense that her feelings match mine."

"Is there an impediment?"

"She craves independence and desires to be the mistress of her own business. You need to understand, she left the brother and family she adores to seek it. She said herself that she admired the spirit of the wagoners, people who left everything behind to make a new life. You and I were born to this country, so we can't fully understand their willingness to sacrifice everything to be here."

Cal scrubbed his beard. "Then don't ask her to marry you."

Michael groaned.

"Right away, that is. Move slowly. Give her time to enjoy her business. But court her. Escort her to church. Take her on picnics, teas, dinners." Cal folded his arms across his chest. "Let her into your life. Take her on walks through our forest. She seemed particularly keen to see a waterfall. Our mountains are difficult to resist. And what about our hot springs?"

The vision of Anne bathing with him in the springs stirred Michael's blood, and he swallowed hard. "Those I will save for when we are married."

"You're right. But don't move too slowly, Michael. You don't want someone else proposing to Anne before you."

Panic slammed into Michael's chest. Mischief danced in his brother's eyes.

"You're joshing me again."

"I am and I do apologize. But I must admit that watching you in your present state, I'm hard pressed not to tease." Cal's expression turned serious. "We've discussed your concerns. May we discuss mine?"

"Of course."

"I'm finding myself attracted to Amelia."

A picture came to mind of Amelia at her most flirtatious. "What!"

"I know what you are thinking, but Amelia has changed greatly since the first time I met her at my wedding in Scotland. She was frivolous, vain, self-important. I think Megan's death and the hardships of the trail made a lasting impression on her. I find her a different creature from the one I knew."

"I understand what you're saying, and upon reflection, I agree. I also think Anne's sweet nature and friendship may have influenced Amelia as well." Michael studied his brother's face. "Something else is bothering you."

"Yes. My wife passed only recently, and I'm weighted with enormous guilt that I have already begun to regard someone else. People in society might think me indecent."

Michael grimaced. "You are the most decent fellow I know."

"Thank you for that. Your good opinion matters more to me than you realize. That is why I am humbled by your example. You mourned Heather for nine years."

Michael hesitated, choosing his words. "That is so, but ours was a true love match. Yours was not."

Cal shrugged. "Honestly, it was not."

Michael stood and rested his hand on Cal's shoulder. "Just as you counseled me, take the relationship slowly. Honor the mourning period, but take advantage of opportunities to know Amelia better...to seek out her feelings for you."

"So...we have answered our problems," Cal said as he moved toward the door.

Michael raised an eyebrow.

"We shall proceed as two tortoises. Slow and steady wins the race."

Michael chortled. "I'm famished. Let's go see what Cookie has for breakfast."

At the house, Cookie was plating two settings with pancakes and sausages. "Good morning, gentlemen. You're just in time."

Michael glanced at the table. "Why only two settings? Where's Cate?"

"She grabbed a pancake and left with Bramble."

Michael's heart tripped. "How long ago? Did she say where she was going?"

Cookie frowned. "She didn't, but she knows not to wander past the sound of the dinner bell. I'll go ring it."

Cal sat at the table. "Come and eat, Michael. Cate is fine. Bramble is with her."

"I don't think I can eat until I know where she is." Michael strode out to the porch steps.

Cal joined him as the clanging of the dinner bell rang through the air. The sound abated and then started again.

"There they are," Cal called out, pointing to the girl and her dog racing across the valley toward home.

Michael's knees trembled as relief flooded through his body. Perhaps he had allowed his daughter too much freedom. He needed a gentle hand to help him rein her in. The sooner the better. Maybe he should move things along faster with Anne than Cal advised.

CHAPTER 19

*C*hecking his cravat for the third time, Michael waited beside the saddled horses for Anne to close the doors to her shop. Following his brother's advice, after sitting beside Anne in church earlier in the day, he had asked her to accompany him to a nearby Cherokee village to meet his friends. The delight on her face as she accepted his invitation confirmed his decision.

The pink ribbons on Anne's hat matched the pink stripes in her bodice and the heightened color in her rosy cheeks.

How had he ever thought of her as plain?

"Good morning, Anne. Did I already mention how lovely you look today?"

He caught the sparkle in her brown eyes before she shyly hooded them. What a darling woman.

Michael drew the smaller mare forward. "This is Cate's horse. She named her Hannah." He chuckled. "Don't ask me why."

"She's a beauty." Anne ran her hand across the horse's neck, and the mare swiveled her head, making eye contact. "We'll have a grand time, won't we, girl?" Anne blew several puffs of air into Hannah's nostrils.

Michael checked the cinch. "I'm afraid I don't own a side-saddle."

"I'm used to cross-saddle. We weren't a rich family, as my father was a barrister. Though we did own two horses, we couldn't afford the luxury of a side-saddle."

She placed her foot into his laced fingers, and he lifted her up and onto the saddle. He helped her slide her boot into the stirrup and arranged her skirts to cover her exposed stockings. The innocent gesture, one he had performed for his wife many times, caused a stronger physical reaction than he had anticipated. He mounted his horse, and soon they headed out of town. At first, neither of them spoke, but simply enjoyed the comfortable quiet.

"How far is the village?" Anne asked, breaking the silence.

"Not far. A couple of miles."

They came to a fork in the road, and he pointed east. "The village is this way."

Anne kept pace and made the turn with ease. "You know these Cherokee well?"

"Yes, I was born here in the mountains. By the way, the ancient Cherokee called them *Shaconage*, which means land of the blue mist. My father was a lumberman and made friends with the villagers when he bought land from them. Growing up, Cal and I visited them often. We would fish and swim and roam the woods for miles."

"Cate comes by it honestly."

He chortled. "I guess so."

"Michael?"

He liked the way she said his name. What a thought. Cal was right. He was a lovelorn clod.

"Yes?"

"How will I communicate with your friends? Do they speak English?"

"Better than most people I know. For generations, missionaries have lived among the Indians, attempting to convert them. First the Moravians, then the Presbyterians and Methodists. There may have been a few Catholics among them. Depending on who taught the Indians English, you can hear German, British, and Scots-Irish accents. It's faint, but it's there."

"So some are Christians?"

"They are. My best friends, John and Henry, are. As are their wives."

"They have white names?"

"John is Onacona or White Owl. Henry is Tsiyi or Canoe. They prefer their white names."

Anne shrugged. "I like the sound of their Cherokee names."

They came upon a thick canebrake with a coal-black dirt trail wide enough for only one horse.

Michael moved ahead. "I'll lead for a short time until we reach the village."

"What are these trees? They're so thick I can't see through them."

Michael pushed one of the limbs out of his way. "It's river-cane. The Cherokee use them for many things—bows and arrows, blowguns, mats. And the women make the most handsome baskets. I think you'll appreciate them."

"It's so much cooler here."

"The trees form a canopy overhead that filters out much of the sun."

The trail widened, opening up to reveal two rows of cabins facing each other across a narrow road that meandered through the village and led downhill to the edge of a river. Cedar shingles topped the roofs of the cabins formed of logs. Groups of women gathered in front of the dwellings. They sat on blankets and grass mats, sewing, weaving baskets, and cooking. Children of all ages ran around them. The youngest ones were naked, exposing their red-brown skin and plump bellies. They laughed and played with uninhibited joy.

Michael waited for Anne to pull up beside him. Two Cherokee men walked toward them, waving their hands. Michael dismounted and helped Anne, who quickly moved close to his side.

He looked down at her upturned face and wide eyes. "There's nothing to fear, Anne. You are with me. You are safe."

"I'm not afraid. I'm amazed. It's like nothing I've ever seen before in my life."

"*Seo*, Michael," the taller of the two men greeted them.

"Seo, John. Henry. This is Anne Forbes. She recently moved to the settlement and has opened a tailor shop." He pressed his hand against the small of Anne's back.

"Seo, Anne," the men said in unison.

Though not as tall as Michael, they carried themselves with confidence and dignity. Muskets rested in the crooks of their arms. Trade shirts that reached to their thighs were cinched in with intricately beaded belts that secured tomahawks at their sides. Their heads were shaved except for top notches they decorated with feathers. They wore breech cloths, leggings, moccasins, and silver bands around their forearms. John carried a knife strapped to his right calf with a strand of rawhide. Strong, imposing men, Michael would never want to come against them in a fight.

With a nod, John led the way through the village to his cabin. A woman, heavy with child, met them at the deerskin-covered doorway.

John gently prodded her toward Anne. "This is my wife, Leah or Brown Bird. She prefers Leah."

Anne curtsied. "It's a pleasure to meet you, Leah."

Leah's lovely face, slightly swollen from her pregnancy,

broke into a smile. She motioned to grass mats, animal skins, and blankets that lay on the ground in front of the cabin. "You will sit?"

Anne helped Leah lower herself atop a pile of deer skins and then settled on a blanket beside her.

Michael nodded toward Leah's burgeoning stomach and said in Cherokee, "You have been busy while I was away, John."

John snorted and then eyed Anne. "You have plans to be busy yourself?"

"I have hopes, but I haven't made my feelings known."

"She is not as beautiful to look at as Heather, but her spirit seems strong...calm."

Anne raised an eyebrow, obviously curious about what they were saying. He looked forward to teaching her the language. He looked forward to teaching her many things.

"Anne, I wish to speak to the men about news I received. Will you be all right without me?"

Anne scrutinized the village, her brown eyes bright with wonder. "I'll be fine."

Farther into the village, several of the men gathered around Michael, greeting him and clapping him on his shoulders.

"I have heard rumblings about a coming fight between the British and the French," Michael began in Cherokee. "They both want the land north of the forks of the Ohio River."

Henry nodded. "It is a place rich with deer and beaver."

"As I said, it's rumor now, but may come to pass. You must be prepared." Michael folded his arms across his chest. "Not only for war, but to choose which side you favor."

"This is not good news, my friend," said John. "We have enough trouble with the Catawba. They have raided many times this season. Not here, but north."

Two women had joined Anne and Leah. They had brought pieces of fabric that Anne bent over to examine. She needed her glasses. She must remember to carry a pair when they were together.

"We'll speak more later," Michael said to the men. "I believe Anne would like to explore your village."

At the cabin, Michael helped Anne to her feet and folded her arm across his. "Let's take a tour."

They came upon a group of men heaping white-hot coals into a long hollowed-out basswood log.

"They're making a canoe," he explained.

Her expressive eyes grew round. "Something as heavy as that will float?"

"See the canoes at the edge of the river? This log will be similar when they have finished with it."

Farther down the path, a handful of young men fashioned darts out of thistle for their blowguns.

"They use the blowguns to hunt small animals...rabbits and squirrels." He motioned to one of them. "Would you show the lady how the blowguns work?"

The youth loaded a dart into a piece of cane, pressed the cane to his mouth, and blew. The dart shot out and embedded into a tree trunk.

Anne clapped her hands. "Fascinating."

Michael enjoyed her reactions to each new discovery and was soon caught up in her contagious enthusiasm. She asked to take part in beadwork, in finger weaving, and stitching deerskins together to make a skirt. She took particular interest in how the women made sewing needles from the legs of deer.

"Why such notice of the needles?" Michael asked.

"Needles are dear," Anne explained. "More valuable than gold, as there are no places in the colonies that make them. I must order them from England."

Michael curled her arm around his. "Let's see more, shall we?"

Anne waved goodbye to the women and let Michael guide her along the trail.

"Look, there." Anne pointed to some men who were practicing archery, taking arrows from quivers, nocking, aiming, and loosing them.

"Look how they've painted animals on the straw targets." Anne pointed to one of the bows and addressed the owner. "May I?"

Despite his obvious curiosity, the man nodded, and some of the others grinned and poked each other's arms.

Michael quickly moved to her side. "Wait. Bows and arrows are dangerous weapons."

She looked up at him and smiled. "It's fine."

The man handed over his bow and arrow. Anne examined the fletching and then took the proper stance. Without seeming to expend much effort, she pulled the bowstring and nocked the arrow. She released the arrow with a loud *thwish*, and it pierced the buffalo painted near the center of the target.

The men gathered around jumped up and down and whooped.

It took a moment for Michael to absorb what he had witnessed. "I'm astonished. I can hardly find the words."

She laughed. "There have been female warriors in Scotland for over five hundred years. That's a fact I used as a young woman to convince William to allow me to learn archery."

Michael shook his head.

Anne handed the bow back to its owner, who said something in Cherokee.

"What did he say?"

"He said the only other woman he has seen hit the target is their Beloved Woman."

She furrowed her brow.

"It's a woman who in her younger days went to war against Cherokee enemies and was known as *War Woman*. Today as a revered warrior, she attends war councils and offers advice. Even Cherokee grandmothers go to her for counsel."

"So it isn't odd for a woman to be a warrior."

"I acknowledge that. I simply wasn't prepared for you—a seamstress, a gentlewoman with a sweet spirit—to be one of them."

The sight of Anne using a bow and arrow would remain with Michael for a long time. How many more fascinating facets were there to this not-so-ordinary woman?

John joined them with a huge grin on his face. "She surprised you, my friend?"

"She did that."

John snorted. "You will come eat with us?"

"I would love that." Anne pressed her hand to her stomach. "I am famished."

At John's cabin, Michael sat on a grass mat next to Anne and John while Leah offered them bean bread wrapped in packets of corn leaves and served on wooden planks.

Anne unwrapped the leaves, exposing a gray-colored loaf. She broke off a bit of the spongy, sweet-smelling bread and took a bite. "Umm. This is delicious. What's in it?"

Michael wiped a crumb of the bread from the corner of her mouth.

"Ground corn, brown beans, fat, and a bit of water," Leah answered and handed two packets to John, who tossed them back and forth to cool them off.

"And what is that boiling in the pot?" Anne asked, breathing in the sweet aroma.

"Kanuchi. It's made from powdered hickory nuts and boiled rice. I will roll the paste into balls tomorrow." She rose up onto her knees and rubbed her back. "I will send you some through Michael." She glanced sidelong at John. "If John doesn't eat them all."

John waggled his eyebrows and then smiled at his wife.

Michael envied the obvious love the couple shared. Could he and Anne have such a marriage? He desired it more with each passing day. He looked up at the sky where the sunlight was growing dim, and shades of pink and orange painted the clouds.

"Anne, as much as I regret it, we must leave. It will be dark soon. I should get you home."

John and his wife walked with them to the entrance of the canebrake, where two men waited with their horses. Leah and Anne hugged and promised to see each other again soon. After Anne mounted, Leah handed her a rivercane basket with red- and blue-dyed diamond patterns.

"It's beautiful." Anne cocked her head. "What's inside?"

"A couple of needles. You liked them, yes?"

Anne examined the needles and dropped them back into the basket. "You are too generous, Leah. I cannot thank you enough."

"Let me carry it." Michael secured it to the back of his saddle.

When they broke through the canebrake and picked up the trail back to the settlement, Anne sighed deeply.

"Why the sigh?"

"Today has been one of the most glorious days of my life. I'm fair tingling with it. Thank you."

"I enjoyed it myself. John and Leah like you very much. You're fine company, Anne."

They had ridden a little farther through a dense stand of trees when Anne pointed toward a huge oak. "That tree reminds me... Are you aware of the family living in a tree near Grace Holler?"

"I am. The Furmans. Why do you ask?"

"It's something Iris said. That they won't accept charity."

"The father is downright pigheaded about it."

"I was trying to think of a way to leave food for them

without being seen." She captured his eyes with hers. "Would you be able to help me find a way?"

How could he resist those lovely eyes?

"I shall put my mind to it."

She rewarded him with a smile so sweet it took everything he had not to sweep her off her horse and into his arms. This courting was going to be more challenging than he anticipated.

CHAPTER 20

*T*he sun had shot its last ray across the sky as Anne stepped outside her shop to greet Michael as he lit a lantern on the side of his buggy.

"Good evening, Michael." Could he hear the thrumming of her heart?

"Good evening. Are you ready for our adventure?" He stood by the carriage ready to assist her.

Anne took his hand but stopped and slightly lifted her petticoats to reveal the toes of her sturdy latchet shoes. "I'm ready. I've tied the laces as tightly as I was able."

He grinned, helped her onto the buggy seat, and slid beside her.

"You brought everything?" she asked, enjoying the warmth of his thigh pressed against hers.

"It's right here behind the seat."

Anne twisted around. "There are three baskets!"

"Cookie insisted on filling each to the brim." Michael slapped the reins and drove them down the street, past the church, and out of town just as the moon began its ascent from behind the mountains.

Anne fiddled with the folds in her outer petticoat. "I'm so excited, I'm shaking. Is this how spies feel when they begin a mission?"

Michael chuckled. "I imagine so."

"How are we to proceed?"

Michael guided the horse onto the narrow road Anne and Iris had taken when they ventured to Grace Holler. "We'll ride as far as we can in the buggy. We'll have to go the rest of the way on foot. We'll go up the mountain, past the path that leads to the Furmans'. I've scouted out a ledge with a view of their front yard. We'll wait there until they've all gone inside for the night."

"We're doing a good thing...are we not, Michael? I wouldn't want to wound their pride."

He curled his fingers over her hand resting in her lap. "Mr. Furman has rebuffed help in the past, but when I was scouting, I could see the dire state of the children. He must come to terms and see that their health and wellbeing far outweigh his pride." He brought the horse to a halt and jumped down. "We'll leave the buggy here."

He secured the horse to a tree, helped Anne down, and retrieved the baskets. "I'll carry the two large ones. Can you carry the other?" He removed his hat and tossed it behind the seat.

Anne draped the basket handle over her arm. "I can. What's in this one?"

"Two of Cookie's pies and a cake."

Anne clapped her hands. "I can imagine the joy on the children's faces."

"Then you'll be even happier to discover a small parcel Cookie packed for us." Michael motioned toward the trail. "This way."

They climbed the steep terrain until Anne's ears popped.

She swallowed hard and tugged on her earlobes as Iris had instructed on their previous walk to the holler.

Michael slowed his pace. "We are nearing the Furmans', so we must tread carefully."

They soon came upon a footpath that cut away from the main trail, through a sparse patch of woods opening to the tree house. Several of the children poked sticks and threw pinecones into a campfire. Anne and Michael skittered past and continued until they reached a formation of boulders. Michael deposited the baskets at the base, opened one, and stuffed a parcel inside his waistcoat. He climbed up on one of the huge rocks and pulled Anne up beside him.

"A few more feet and then we'll have to crawl to the edge." He paused. "Can you manage?"

The bright full moon lit his face. A tendril of his hair had come loose from the rawhide string. Anne could not resist and tucked it behind his ear. "I'll follow your lead."

Michael dropped on all fours and started to crawl. She copied him and made her way close to him at the ledge.

In the distance, the outline of the church steeple stood out against the trees surrounding the town. Candles and lanterns glowed in the windows of buildings and houses.

Her pulse pounded in her throat. "We're higher up than I expected," she whispered.

He threw his arm across her waist. "You're safe with me. I won't let any harm come to you," he whispered back.

The Furmans continued to gather around the campfire. One of the children had climbed onto his mother's lap and had fallen asleep.

"We may have to wait some time." Michael sat up, opened the parcel he had been carrying, and handed Anne a piece of cake.

"What a delightful surprise." Anne took a bite. "It tastes wonderful. I know how much you'll love it."

"What makes you say that?"

"Cate let me in on the fact that you and Cal have a sweet tooth. She shared how you and he used to fight over sweets."

"Ha! So Cate is sharing our family secrets. She likes you."

"I do hope so, because I have come to care for her."

"I can't tell you how much that pleases me."

When they finished eating, Michael lay on his back with his arms crossed and his hands pillowing his head. Anne did the same.

How natural it felt lying beside him.

"It's nice here with you, Anne."

His low, sensual voice sent her senses into chaos.

They remained silent, lulled by the nocturnal sounds surrounding them—the dancing of a stream over rocks, the breeze ruffling through treetops, the dwindling call of cicadas turning in for the night, the distant howling of a wolf.

Anne rose up on her elbows. "I thought the night would be quiet. I'm amazed. It's like a symphony."

He leaned up next to her. "Do you hear that?"

Anne cocked her head. "An owl?"

"Yes. It's a great horned owl. I know because their hoots come in threes. Usually the female calls first, then the male, and then they hoot together on the third. You can imitate them and they will call back." He chuckled. "Obviously, since we're lying low, I won't demonstrate now, but we'll come back out here again. There are so many things I want to share with you."

"I should like that." Her heart yearned for any time to be near him.

"The stars are popping out." He rolled over and scanned the Furmans' yard. "I think they have finally retired for the night. Let's go."

They crawled away from the ledge until they could safely stand. He spanned her waist with his hands and lifted her from the boulder.

"The stars are reflected in your eyes, Anne. Have I ever told you how much the color of them reminds me of the white oak acorns so favored by mountain deer?" He kissed her eyelids. "Coffee shades with amber flecks."

Anne kept her eyelids closed as his words and the warmth of lips ignited fires throughout her body.

He cleared his throat and stepped away. "Let's get on with our mission, shall we?"

A bit dazed, Anne shook her head and followed him until he stopped and then headed down the footpath toward the tree house. Slowly, stealthily, they inched their way to the edge of the clearing where they deposited the baskets.

They turned around and had almost reached the mountain path when a man yelled, "Who goes there? Speak up or I'll shoot."

Michael pressed his hand against Anne's back. "Run!" he rasped.

With Michael behind her, Anne took off running so fast, her feet barely touched the ground. A musket shot rang out, but her throat had tightened, stifling her scream. Another shot echoed across the mountain, sending shards of terror up her spine. Suddenly, the muscles in her side gripped hard, forcing her to stop.

"Michael! A stitch...in my side. The pain. I cannot move."

He swept her up into his arms and carried her the rest of the way to the buggy, where he sat on a fallen tree trunk and held her in his lap.

"Where does it hurt, dear one?"

"Here." Anne rubbed her side. "But it's already abating."

"May I help?"

She nodded and lay still as he massaged the muscles in her side where a tingling soon replaced the pain. He sat quietly until her ragged breathing calmed. The moon shone on his face, lighting his eyes that held a strange glow. His lips twitched.

"Something amuses you, Michael?"

"I'm sorry, love, but I cannot help thinking about the last time I told you to run."

It took a moment, especially considering that unexpected endearment he had thrown in, but Anne finally remembered the skunk. A giggle rose up inside of her, and then she recalled her breakneck scramble down the path.

She laughed. "I must have been a sight."

"No. You continue to amaze me. Not only can you fashion beautiful clothing, you can shoot a bow and arrow and run like the wind. Life with you is turning out to be quite pleasant, Anne."

What a stirring sentiment, but not as thrilling as his calling her *love*. Would they share more adventures and laughter? Oh, she hoped so.

CHAPTER 21

$\mathcal{A}$nne leaned into the work table and peeked out the display window. Katherine and Christopher waited by the entrance, their expressions eager, excited. The twins had pinned on the dark-blue aprons she had fashioned for them. She ran her hands down her bodice and pressed the creases of her petticoats, the same hue as her assistants' aprons.

Opening day had finally arrived. There was not one inch of the shop that had not been cleaned or polished. Two chairs and a small table rested on a blue hook rug in front of the window that displayed the gentlemen dolls. A vase with bright yellow daisies decorated the table, creating a tableau to entice patrons to linger and converse. Next to the work table and shelves of material, a desk awaited the writing of receipts and orders and noting appointments.

"There's a crowd. Small, but a crowd." Anne's pulse raced. "You may open the doors."

Iris and Amelia led the others inside.

Iris' curious glances darted here and there around the room. "A triumph, dear girl."

"I couldn't have done it without you." Anne hugged her. "Thank you."

"You are most welcome." She motioned to one of the cushioned chairs. "I shall sit there and watch the proceedings."

Amelia clasped Anne's hand. "I'm so proud of you, my friend. I'm determined to be the first to place an order. I have spied some material on the second shelf there that will make a lovely dress." She made a beeline for the shelf and was soon in conversation with Katherine.

Four couples Anne had met in church filed through the doorway.

One of the ladies toted a length of blue-striped cloth over her arm. "I want to speak to you about making a dress for me with this."

Anne felt the cotton, an expensive material difficult to come by. "It's a fine color that will complement your eyes. If you wait with Mrs. Clarendon, I'll be with you in a moment."

Next, Anne greeted a gentleman and his wife unfamiliar to her.

"We are Mr. and Mrs. Wells," the man said, "and we would speak to you about tailoring clothes for our son, who will be leaving in three months to attend medical school in London. Of course, he will purchase more clothing while there, but we mean for him to arrive properly attired. We have Mr. Harrigan's assurance that you can meet our needs in an excellent manner."

Anne curtsied to them.

Bless Michael. Once again, he showed support for her.

The amount of work for such a commission would test her, but she would rise to the challenge. "I thank you for your confidence in me. If you would, please see my assistant, Katherine, and she will arrange an appointment to take your son's measurements."

Anne welcomed each visitor warmly but searched behind

them until she spotted the face she most wanted to see. How handsome Michael looked in his finely tailored coat. He wore a jabot instead of a cravat. Had he donned his more formal attire in honor of her special occasion?

What a dear, thoughtful man.

They had not seen each other since their mission for the Furmans two days prior. She had missed him but did not realize how much until she saw him again.

He entered the shop holding Cate's hand. "Congratulations, Anne. You've done well. I know how hard you've worked for this."

His praise warmed her, as did the light in his hazel eyes. "Thank you, but I didn't do it alone. I had a great deal of help."

"Congratulations, Anne," Cate chimed in, her eyes wide with curiosity. "Papa, may I look through the ribbons?"

"Certainly." He gazed at his daughter with heartwarming adoration.

Anne longed for the day he would regard her with equal feeling.

"Michael, about our visit with your Cherokee friends..." She locked eyes with his. "I have thought much about that day and the lovely people. I particularly want to speak to you about their handworks and crafts and hear your opinion about an idea I have. I know you are busy, but could you find time to speak about it?"

"I'd enjoy nothing more. Would you care to take a tour of my sawmill? Say, this Sunday after the service?" He acknowledged Mr. Wells with a nod. "Although from what I'm observing today, you may be too busy."

Katherine was talking with a female customer and writing in the appointment book. Christopher had escorted a gentleman into the back room to take his measurements for a waistcoat. Anne would be very busy, but wasn't that what she had hoped and prayed for? Or was loving Michael already changing her outlook on her dreams?

"I would love to tour the mill, and Sunday is ideal."

Michael bowed. "I'll leave you to your customers and look forward to seeing you Sunday."

Later that evening, Anne said goodbye to the last customer and dismissed Katherine and Christopher with her heartfelt praise. She closed and locked the front doors and doused the lanterns placed around the room. Holding a lantern high, she recalled the evening—the lively, pleasant conversations and the contentment on people's faces. The opening had been a great success. She breathed a heavy sigh. Much work lay ahead. She bowed her head and thanked God for His many blessings, for bringing her to Graniteville, for the friends she had made, and for the hopes of a deep and abiding love shared with Michael.

If only her family had been here to attend the opening. Had David grown much in the past weeks and was he missing his brother as much as she? Though it might be weeks before William and Gail arrived home, she decided to write and describe Graniteville and its people and tell them of her success. Maybe, one day, Gail would rethink her decision and agree to return to the colonies.

CHAPTER 22

Outside the church, with Michael at her side, Anne waved goodbye to Iris and Amelia as they walked away chatting with a group of parishioners.

From her place on the seat of a wagon loaded with lumbermen, Cate waved and shouted, "Goodbye, Papa and Anne."

Anne waved back and walked with Michael to his buggy. "Cate isn't coming with us?"

"No, she's going ahead to help Cookie serve the men their lunch." He handed Anne into the buggy and sat beside her. He slapped the reins and guided the horse away from the church toward the main street.

"I thought we were going to your mill."

Michael looked down at the tips of her heeled silk shoes. "We are. But I have a surprise, and to see it, you must wear more serviceable shoes."

When they reached Anne's shop, she hurried upstairs and donned a pair of leather latchet shoes. In her excitement, she could barely tie the laces. Before leaving, she glanced about her quarters that she had transformed into a cozy nest—gauze curtains that billowed in the breeze and let in an abundance of

SUSAN F. CRAFT

sunshine, the rocker where she read her Bible, the sweet aroma
emanating from the vase filled with lavender and white flox.
She closed the door behind her and ran back down the stairs.
Halfway to the front doors, she remembered the shirts she had
made and grabbed the packages from the work table.

Outside, she lifted the hem of her petticoats. "Will
these do?"

"Yes, but let me retie this one so you don't trip." He stored his
hat behind the buggy seat, bent down on one knee, and tightened
the lace on her shoe. The intimate gesture made Anne's heart skip.
How nice it would be to lean down and kiss the back of his neck.

When he stood, she handed him the packages wrapped in
brown paper, and he raised an eyebrow.

"The shirts I promised Mr. Craig and Mr. Gibbons."

"Ah." He placed the packages on the floor of the buggy and
helped Anne up onto the seat.

Tucked so closely next to Michael inside the covered buggy,
the faint aroma of limes tickled her nose. The roof of the buggy
not only created a cozy feeling, it sheltered them from the
already blistering sun.

"When does the weather begin to cool here?"

Michael retrieved his hat and donned it. "Not for another
month. The first things you'll detect will be cooler nights and
the absence of bugs."

"I haven't noticed many bugs, except for spiders. Ach." She
shivered. "I could well do weeout them."

Michael chuckled. "Did you realize that when you're out of
countenance or emotional, your Scots accent comes out?"

"I did not."

They shared a glance. It would take only the slightest lean
to feel his lips against hers. A tension stirred her insides, and
she quickly drew her attention to the road as they traversed out
of town. At a fork in the road, Michael guided them east toward

the Cherokee village. A few minutes later, he took another fork west.

Anne studied the forest. "There's a distinct change here, but I cannot pinpoint it."

"You're observant. Although the trees are dense, there's hardly any underbrush. We try to keep it cut back within a large perimeter of the mill. If there's ever a fire, that will help keep it from spreading."

As he finished his explanation, a log structure surrounded by a cluster of several smaller ones came into view. Between the buildings, a thin layer of pine needles blanketed the pristine grounds almost devoid of trees. Michael halted the buggy in front of an unpainted clapboard building. He jumped down, assisted Anne as she stepped down, and then tucked her hand into the crook of his elbow.

"This is the office. I can see my brother through the window."

When they entered the building, Cal sprang up from a desk that took up most of the room. "Anne, what a delight." He bowed. "We've been sprucing up in your honor. Usually this desk is flooded with papers."

"I'm the one who is delighted." Anne curtsied. "I've been uncommonly eager to discover how a sawmill works."

Truth be told, she wanted to see where Michael spent a good deal of his time—a way of picturing him when they were apart.

"As you see, this is our office, though neither of us spends much time here." Cal motioned toward the door. "What next, Michael? The bunkhouse? It will be empty while the men are finishing their lunch."

They left the office for a log structure with a porch that spanned the front with chairs and crates scattered across it.

Inside, Michael swept out his arm. "This is where the men

sleep. That long bench, there, is where they play cards and socialize."

"That's a deacon seat," Anne said. "I remember the one you fashioned for us at the shelter for the smallpox patients."

Cal glanced away.

Anne touched his forearm. "I am sorry, Cal. I didn't mean to bring you pain."

"Don't worry yourself, Anne. I'm fine."

Michael pressed his hand to the small of Anne's back. The warmth of his fingertips comforted her.

Cal stepped into the middle of the room. "The bunkhouse can accommodate up to sixty men."

"There are only twenty here today. But we'll reach capacity in a couple of weeks when we start the fall harvesting of oaks, maples, and hickory trees," Michael added.

"The men sleep two to a bunk," Cal continued. "The mattresses are prickly since they are stuffed with hay. They line the bunks with cedar boughs."

"For the nice smell?" Anne looked up at Michael.

His eyes sparkled. "No. Not for the nice smell. It's to keep away bedbugs and greybacks...lice."

"Ugh. I regret asking."

Cal and Michael chuckled.

Anne approached a dulcimer lying on one of the mattresses. "What a beautiful instrument."

"It belongs to Mr. Trent. Our town carpenter made it from basswood that we provided." Michael plucked one of the strings. "I'm eager for you to hear Trent play."

"I look forward to it."

Another time to be near Michael. More and more, she desired to be nowhere else. His mere presence brought her senses to life.

"See there, on the bench? It's a carving of a dog, and it looks like Bramble." She examined the figurine the size of her palm. "It's fine workmanship. As fine as any I've seen."

"It's Mr. Craig's work," said Michael.

"That reminds me. My packages. Will you get them for me, Michael?"

"Certainly."

When Michael left, Anne looked at Cal. "You both love this place a great deal. I sense it."

"It's been our life since the day we were born." His expression grew serious. "My brother is a fine man, Anne."

"Yes, I know."

"And you are a fine woman."

She looked away, avoiding eye contact. Why was Cal saying such things?

"I have the packages," Michael called out from the doorway as he slipped them under his arm.

"Let's proceed to the dining room, shall we?" Cal led them through the back door and into a room crowded with men sitting at tables finishing their meals.

The moment the men spotted them, they jump up from their chairs.

"Be seated." Michael motioned to Anne. "This is Miss Forbes. Many of you have seen her in town or at church. She's honoring us with her presence today on a tour of our mill."

The men bowed and sat back down.

Anne leaned close to Michael and whispered, "Would you give Mr. Craig and Mr. Gibbons their shirts? It would be more proper coming from you."

"I don't agree but will do as you ask." Michael stepped forward. "Craig, Gibbons...Miss Forbes has something for you. In appreciation for helping her with her tailor shop."

The men opened the packages and held up the shirts.

"Thank you, Miss Forbes, I'll wear it tomorrow." Mr. Craig examined the stitches. "Mighty good workmanship."

"Coming from you, Mr. Craig, that is a fine compliment. I saw your carving of Bramble."

Hearing his name, the hound dog rose up, stretched, and then sniffed around Anne's hem. He leaned against her as if inviting her to scratch his ears, which she did.

Cookie, Cate, and two men who must have been assistants entered the dining hall. Cate wore her lumbermen clothes with an apron pinned to the front. Tendrils of her hair had escaped her knitted cap and framed her face flushed from the heat of the kitchen.

"Isn't she adorable," Anne said in a low voice.

Michael beamed. "She is that."

Cookie nodded at Anne. "Welcome, Miss Forbes. Happy to see you. I'd invite you to my kitchen, but it's not presentable at the moment."

Anne nodded back. "Maybe another time."

Cookie clapped his hands. "All right, men, you're well past your twenty minutes. Haul yourselves out of here so we can get this place prepared for supper."

Several of the men downed the last of their coffee and scrambled out the back door behind the others.

Cate walked across the room. "It's a pleasure to see you again."

To Anne's surprise, the girl wrapped her arms around her waist and gave her a hug.

Anne gently pulled Cate's braid back over her shoulder and straightened her knit cap. "It's nice to see you."

Cate's greeting warmed Anne's heart. She had come to love the young lady.

Cookie spoke to one of his assistants who had left and returned with a basket. "As you requested, I prepared a picnic lunch for you, Mr. Harrigan. The rest of you, back to the kitchen."

Cate shrugged and followed the men through the door.

"Thank you, Cookie." Michael slipped one arm through the basket handle. "This way, Anne. We'll see you later, Cal."

"Have a pleasant time." Cal waved as Anne and Michael left the building.

Outside, walking shoulder to shoulder, they followed a wide path leading away from the bunkhouse. Michael's large hand engulfed hers, his calluses rough but warm. They passed a shelter full of hundreds of vertical stacks of planks.

"That's where we store the newly hewn planks until they air dry. It will take several months before they can be used for building. We'll wait until late fall or winter to harvest oaks, maples, and hickory trees."

A handful of men had gathered in an open area sheltered by a wooden plank roof. The grinding of a saw against wood and the aroma of freshly cut cedar filled the air. One man, wearing a straw hat completely encrusted with sawdust, climbed out of a deep hole in the ground and brushed wood chips from his clothes.

"That's our pit saw. I would show it to you, but I am famished." Michael cocked his head. "Another time, yes?"

"I'd like that. And I'm hungry too."

They left the road and moved onto a footpath that led to the edge of a lake. Michael retrieved a blanket from the basket, and the two of them spread it on the ground. He lay down and propped up on his elbows. Anne sat beside him, arranged her petticoats over her legs, and explored the basket.

"There's bread and slices of ham and cheese, some scrumptious-looking pickles, and blueberries." Anne popped a morsel of bread into her mouth. "Mm-m. It's still warm from the oven."

He leaned forward, and she fed him a piece of bread, drawing in a breath as his tongue touched her fingers. When they had finished feasting on the food, they watched a flock of geese land on the far end of the lake.

"In a few weeks, this entire lake will be full of logs that have been floated down the river from our logging camps."

"That must be a sight to behold. But doesn't the water ruin the logs?"

"On the contrary. It helps preserve the wood and cleans it too." He pointed to the lake. "You'd be surprised to know that there are logs...called sinker logs...at the bottom of this water that have been there for decades as fresh as the day they were felled. The freezing water has preserved them."

Amazed, Anne shook her head.

He helped her up to stand beside him. "And now, for your surprise."

CHAPTER 23

$\mathcal{A}$nne's mind worked to absorb all she had seen and heard. There was more?

"This way." He led them back out to the road.

"The picnic things?"

"Leave them. We'll pick them up on the way back."

As they started walking, he held her hand. Once more, Anne knew the joy of connecting with him.

"Michael?"

"Hmm?"

"Do you remember when I said there is something I want your opinion on concerning your Cherokee friends?"

"I do."

"The beadwork and hand weaving the women do...it's quite beautiful. Do they sell them?"

"They do, especially their baskets. They sell them mostly at trading posts."

"I was thinking I could somehow add the beadwork to my dress designs."

"Yes?" He maneuvered her past a pine branch protruding from the edge of the road.

"I would use them to decorate the fancier gowns. Once I've thought through what I plan to do, would you help me address the Cherokee? Perhaps help me decide how much to pay them for their work?"

"I'd be honored." He squeezed her fingers. "It's a marvelous idea."

They came to a place in the road where six pathways of various sizes converged. Several dormant campfires lay in a circle.

Puzzled, Anne looked to Michael.

"It's called a dancing ground. Once every month or so, the people who use these paths gather here at midnight to dance, sing, and play music. The strumming of dulcimers and mandolins can lift your spirits or send you into a time of melancholy." He stared off into the forest. "The best part for me is the storytelling. Many a night, I've sat completely enthralled by tales of mountain folks."

"Would you bring me here for that, Michael?"

"Be assured of it." He motioned to one of the footpaths. "But for now, it's time for your surprise."

They had not traveled far when Anne heard a rumbling sound. "The waterfall?"

Michael beamed. "You said you had always wanted to see one."

They broke through the trees to the sight of not one, but two layers of water that fanned out and tumbled over huge boulders and into a small basin. Anne ran toward the edge of the pool where the water spilled out into a shallow stream and gurgled over stacks of rocks, miniature versions of the larger waterfall.

She pulled off her straw hat, and throwing her arms open wide, she twirled around. "It's beautiful."

Michael swept her up, and cradling her in his arms, he whirled them around until they both laughed with abandon.

He stood still and locked eyes with hers. "Do you have any idea how many times I have desired to scoop you up and hold you like this?"

"As many times as I wished it."

He dipped his head and captured her lips with his. She dropped her hat on the ground, clasped her arms about his neck, and gave herself over to the longings that shot through her. She wanted closer...more. Shuddering, he broke the kiss, slid her down his body, and gently placed her feet on the ground. He pressed her head to his chest, and his heart thundered beneath her ear.

He stepped back, resting his hands on her hips. "I knew kissing you would be...wonderful. But this..."—he twirled a tendril of her hair around his finger—"is more than I ever dreamed."

She could not agree more, but judging from the desire in his eyes, she would be wise not to express it just now.

He guided her to sit on a boulder beside the stream. "Anne, we haven't known each other long. But if I knew you a hundred more years, I don't think my feelings would be any stronger. My dear heart, would you do me the honor of being my wife?"

So many thoughts ran through Anne's mind that she found it difficult to respond.

He furrowed his brow. "Why do you hesitate? You do not feel the same?"

"Yes, yes." She swallowed hard. "I'm overjoyed. So much so...I'm finding it difficult to speak."

"Ha! You worried me for a moment." He sat beside her and pulled her onto his lap.

She twisted in his arms and caressed his beard. "When did you know...that you love me?"

"There was something...a connection of sorts that I felt the moment I saw you. You can't imagine how I felt when I discovered you weren't married. At first, I thought of you as a friend.

But the more I saw you—your courage to leave your family to explore a new life, your kind and loving spirit, the way you treat my Cate—the more I wanted to be with you." He slid her hand from his beard and kissed her palm. "There were times when we were apart that I ached...I missed you so."

Anne trembled with delight with his every word. She slid her arm around his back and rested her head against his neck.

"And then, there was the way you cared for the sick, covered in who knows what and the sweat-damp tendrils of hair around your smudged face"—he laughed—"and the time with the skunk...and the way the spectacles enlarge your lovely brown eyes..."

"But I was so bedraggled all those times."

"They are most endearing to me."

Did he truly adore those things about her that embarrassed her and made her feel less attractive compared to Heather?

He kissed the base of her neck. "What a lovely spot. I cannot wait to discover more places to kiss."

Anne sucked in a breath and felt her face grow hot.

"You are shy, my darling. I mustn't suggest such things to you yet." He lifted her hand to his lips, caressed it and then her fingertips.

His mouth left warm places on her skin as if he marked them as his own. The gesture was intoxicating and made Anne lightheaded.

"When shall we marry? I cannot wait to share our home and spend our days exploring the mountains and forests. There are so many more waterfalls to show you."

He spoke of days together. Anne stiffened. "What of my shop?"

Michael tucked in his chin. "You do not expect to keep working?"

Anne slid off his lap and clutched her hands behind her

back. "I thought you understood. It is my dream. Something I've longed for most of my life."

He frowned. "Be reasonable, Anne. You work twelve hours a day, six days a week. More than that, if you count the hours you spend after you close."

"How do you know?"

"I cannot count the times I rode past your shop late at night only to discover you next to a lantern hunched over your work." He raked his hand through his hair. "I cannot imagine what you are thinking, Anne. What time would be left for us as man and wife? What of our children?"

There it was...the choice. Michael or her work? She knew this would present itself, but she had deliberately avoided it. She had once held a piece of rare satin in her hands, made a wrong cut, and damaged it beyond repair. Would she repeat that mistake with this life-changing decision? She loved the man with all of her being. But what of her dreams?

She recalled her brother and his sacrifice for his wife. Was she being selfish? *Lord, help me. I am confused.*

She held her arms out to him. "I beseech you, I need time."

"Time for what? To decide that you love your profession more than you love me? The idea of it hurts...and angers me." He stomped away, and over his shoulder he called out, "Come, let's get back."

Anne picked up her hat and followed him, but he strode so fast, she found it difficult to keep up. She had caused him pain, and it made her sick to her stomach. They passed the picnic spot. The plates and basket lay abandoned, scattered, just as her lovely memories. At the pit saw, Michael raced by, ignoring the men's greetings. Finally, they reached the office where Cal waited outside.

Michael stopped long enough to ask, "Cal, would you see Anne back to her home, please?"

Anne waited until he moved out of sight around the bunkhouse before she broke into sobs that racked her body.

"What has happened?" Cal put his arm over her shoulder.

"I-I-I canno speak to it. I am fashed. Undone." She pulled off her mobcap and pressed it to her face, trying desperately to muffle her weeping.

Cal glanced around, but the yard was empty. "Let's get you to the buggy."

Anne cried off and on the entire way home and was so spent when they arrived, she could hardly step out of the buggy on her own.

Cal wrapped his arm around her. "Shall I help you inside?"

"Aye...please. I'm feeling poorly."

Leaning heavily on Cal, she waited for him to open the door and escort her to the bottom of the stairs leading to her room. "I can make it upstairs, if you would be so kind as to close the shop doors."

Cal's usually cheerful eyes clouded. "Are you certain? I will stay with you if you need me."

"You are a dear..." Her voice cracked. "But I'll manage."

"All right. I cannot imagine what happened between you and my brother. Would you care to share with me? I'm a good listener."

"I appreciate it, Cal, but I am simply not up to it."

Cal's shoulders drooped. "God bless you, Anne."

He left, closing the doors behind him.

"God help me," she whispered and ascended the steps.

CHAPTER 24

The three days following Michael's confrontation with Anne were torture. He roamed around the sawmill as a bear with a thorn in its paw. When he was not barking orders, he hardly spoke to anyone.

In a stunted conversation, he had given Cal an account of what had occurred. When his daughter constantly questioned him about Anne, he asked Cal to tell her only that he and Anne were busy and would not be seeing each other for a while. It was cowardly to leave it to Cal, but he could not face Cate and her relentless inquiries. Besides, speaking the truth aloud would be agonizing.

On the pretense of checking the lake before the logs moved downriver, he visited the place where he and Anne had picnicked. He recalled her modest efforts to cover her legs with her skirts as they sat together on the blanket. Remembering the warmth of her fingers as she fed him a piece of bread, he ran his fingers across his mouth. He could not bring himself to go back to the waterfall. Too many disturbing memories there.

The morning of the third day since Anne had broken his heart—is that how he would measure time now?—Michael and

Cal met at the breakfast table. Cookie entered with a tray of eggs, bacon, and scones. Cate had not joined them.

"Cookie, has Cate gone exploring again?"

"I'm afraid she has. I made her take a scone on her way out." Cookie clasped his thumbs underneath his apron. "Bramble went with her."

Relieved by that news, Michael shrugged. "Sometimes I think that dog has more sense than my daughter."

"How long ago did she leave?" Cal asked.

"It's more than a half hour now." Cookie looked back and forth at the brothers, who frowned at each other. "I'll ring the dinner bell."

Michael and Cal went to the front porch, where Michael let out a shrill whistle. "She knows she's not supposed to go past the sound of my whistle."

The clanging of the bell echoed through the yard.

Michael paced the porch.

Cal scanned the valley. "No sign of Cate or Bramble."

"Too much time has passed." Michael took the front steps two at the time. "I'm going to search."

Cal started to follow. "I'll go with you."

"No, you stay here in case she comes back. Then come and find me."

Michael hurried to the stables, saddled his horse, and rode across the front of the house. "I know all the trees she likes to climb. I'll search there first," he yelled out to Cal.

Traveling from one stand of trees to the next, Michael sought out Cate's favorite places to explore. His shrill whistle echoed through the forest but was met with silence. Surely, if something had happened, Bramble would respond.

Dejected, he headed back to the house and met Cal on the porch.

"Did she return home?" Michael's pulse raced.

"No." Cal leaned on the porch rail. "You think she may have gone into town?"

"She is supposed to ask permission." Michael pulled off his tricorn and clenched its brim. "She wasn't content with the explanations about Anne. Maybe she went to see her. I'll check."

Cal descended the steps. "I'll go to the mill and make ready the men...just in case."

The trip to town seemed to take more time than ever. Since the boarding house was closest, Michael entered the front door, where Iris greeted him warmly.

"Is Cate here, Iris?" He prayed she would say *yes*.

Iris frowned. "No, she hasn't been here today. Is something amiss?"

"No one has seen her in a while. I'm worried."

Iris patted his shoulder. "You'll find her. Maybe she's with Anne. You know now much she likes her."

Hope rose in Michael's heart, and he made straight for Anne's shop. He entered and found her sitting alone in a chair, sewing on a piece of material. She glanced up at him, her eyes magnified by the glasses perched on the end of her nose. They were puffy. Had she been crying?

"Michael!" She stood up so fast, the material dropped to the floor.

He recognized the fabric Anne and he had chosen for Cate's dress. Would he ever see his precious girl wear it? He sucked in a painful breath.

"I'm sorry, Anne. I don't have time to speak with you. Have you seen Cate?"

"Not today. What's wrong? You look terribly anxious."

His shoulders drooped. "I cannot find her. I've looked every-where." He choked on the last words.

Please, Lord, please, let my baby be safe.

He must not allow his emotions to reign. He had to keep his wits about him.

Anne clasped his forearm. "How long since you've seen her?"

"Since very early this morning." He started to leave. "I've got to get back out there." He hurried outside and bolted up onto his horse without the need of a stirrup.

Anne approached him. "Please, may I go with you?

When he did not answer straight away, she put her hand on his knee. "Please, Michael, I want to help. I love her too."

He held out his forearm, and she grabbed it, allowing him to pull her up onto the saddle in front of him. He pressed her back tighter against him and took the reins. Having his arms around her brought him comfort.

"Where are we going?"

"To search the forest around the house once more." He prodded the horse, and they took off at a gallop.

Neither of them spoke. Halfway down the road to his house, Michael spotted his Cherokee friends John and Henry riding their horses toward town.

"Seo," John called out and waved.

Michael pulled up beside them. "I need your help. I can't find Cate. I've searched all the places I know."

"What can we do?" Henry asked.

"We must search the forest around the house. Cate loves to climb trees. I searched once but may have missed her."

John and Henry were turning their horses toward Michael's house when Anne quickly twisted around.

"Wait." She looked up at Michael. "I remember a conversation with Cate, when we were having tea at the mercantile. She mentioned one particular tree..." She scrubbed her forehead with her fingers. "Something about a giant black willow growing beside a waterfall. She mentioned that it's so tall, it's frightening and so far from your house you wouldn't like it if she went there."

"I know it. I know the very tree!" Michael shouted and kicked the horse's sides.

John and Henry followed. They had galloped about a half mile when the sound of water cascading over rocks resounded through the forest.

Michael clasped his arms closer around Anne and whistled.

"Did you hear that?" John sat up on his horse. "It sounded like a howl."

Michael whistled again and heard the howl. "It's Bramble," he yelled and guided his horse toward the sound.

They came upon Bramble pacing up and down at the base of a black willow tree. John helped Anne from the horse. Michael dismounted and ran to the tree. His heart thundering as loud as the waterfall, he leaned against the trunk and searched up through the limbs. There, up near the top, Cate barely clung to a Y-shaped branch, her legs dangling in the air.

"Cate! Papa's here. I'm coming to get you." He ripped his hat from his head, sprang up, and hauled himself onto the lowest branch. Carefully choosing strategic handholds, he made his way toward his daughter. He gripped limb after limb and pushed aside branches that swatted him in the face, bringing tears to his eyes. Several times his feet slipped, and he would have fallen if he had not hugged the trunk. Once, the branches and twigs above were so matted, he lost sight of Cate.

How had his petite daughter managed the perilous climb? A shaft of admiration tugged his heart.

"I'm almost there, Kitten. How are you?"

"F-fine, now that you're here," Cate called out and then started crying. "Oh, Papa, I'm so very sorry."

Michael hiked himself onto the limb just below her. Seeing her face lifted the heavy weight from his chest, and he took a deep breath for the first time in hours. "Not to worry, my darling girl. Are you hurt?"

"My shoulder hurts terribly." She shuddered. "I fell from a limb near the top."

Michael's shudder matched hers.

Cate whimpered. "Poor Bramble has been beside himself. I think he wanted to go for help but didn't want to leave me. Will he be all right?"

"I'm sure he will be fine. Now, let's see how we can get you down without hurting you. Which shoulder is it?"

"Th-the right."

He reached out and ran his hand across her shoulder and back.

Cate moaned and her face paled. Michael's stomach lurched as if someone struck him.

He called down to John, Henry, and Anne, "She hurt her shoulder, but I don't think it's broken. It's dislocated. I'll get her down first, and then we'll fix that."

For the first time since reaching near the top of the tree, Michael looked out from his vantage, took note of the astonishing height, and gulped. How best to get them both down safely and without hurting Cate? It would be tricky.

John climbed the lower branches and held out a rope. "Will you need this?"

"No. I'm going to carry her." Michael studied the nearest branches, searching for the best way back down.

"All right, darling girl, Papa is moving over to you on that limb just underneath you." He pointed to the spot. "I'll slide you onto my back. Hold onto my neck with your left arm and wrap your legs around my waist. Can you do that?"

"Yes, Papa."

He winked at her. "That's my brave girl."

Moving slowly, carefully, Michael maneuvered Cate onto his back. She cried out but held on tight. Limb by limb, they made their way down, stopping once for him to get a better grip on her. When they reached the bottom limb, John and Henry held out their arms.

"You can let go of me, Cate. My friends won't let you fall."

She loosened her stranglehold, and Michael gently released her to John, who laid her on the ground. Bramble whined and tried to get close.

"All is well, Bramble." Anne patted the dog's head and pointed to the trunk of the tree. "Sit there."

Bramble obeyed but kept a close watch.

Anne dropped to her knees beside Cate. "Praise the Lord you are safe, precious girl."

Michael swung down from the last limb and sat beside Anne. He took out his kerchief and wiped streaks of blood from Cate's face and neck. "I'm going to fix your arm, Kitten. I'll have to pull on it very hard, and it will hurt terribly at first. But I assure you, most of the pain will go away once we have your shoulder in place. Do you trust me?"

"Of course, Papa."

His daughter's love and confidence made tears well in Michael's eyes. He scrubbed them away with his thumb. "Anne, will you go to her other side? Hold her hand and keep her attention? John, if you would steady her shoulder."

Anne positioned herself next to Cate, whose face had turned white as the clouds overhead. "You hurt your arm, but I see some cuts and bruises. Can you tell me where it pains you most, lass?"

Cate started to answer, but her scream drowned out the loud popping and grinding noises as Michael moved her arm back into place.

Sweat popped out on Michael's brow, and he leaned down and kissed Cate's cheek. "It's done. You should feel much better now."

Anne handed him her kerchief. He wiped his brow and

then locked eyes with hers. He tucked the kerchief into his waistcoat and mouthed *thank you*. Anne was the very definition of a help mate. She wore a mantle of calm and comfort wherever she went, and he truly appreciated her presence.

Henry poked John's back. "We make a travois."

As the men gathered straight limbs and fashioned them into a sled with blankets from their horses, Anne and Michael examined the abrasions on Cate's body.

"Thank heavens, they are all surface, but we must get them cleaned soon," Anne said.

They attached the travois to Michael's horse and then transferred Cate onto it. Anne rode behind John on his horse as he led the way back to the house. Michael followed, then Henry. Bramble lumbered alongside the travois. A sentinel, remaining at his post.

The trek took less than an hour. The moment he spotted them, Cal, who had been waiting on the porch with several of the lumbermen, ran down the steps and held Cate's hand. "Thank the good Lord. You gave your Uncle Cal a terrible scare."

"I am sorry to have caused everyone so much trouble," Cate said with trembling lips.

"You mustn't fash yourself," Anne said as Henry helped her dismount.

Michael swept his daughter into his arms, then carried her up the stairs and to her room, where he laid her on her mattress. Bramble positioned himself on the floor at the foot of the bed.

"I'll need a tub of hot water. A pail. Drying cloths, bandages, and ointment." Anne looked at Cal, John, Henry, and Cookie loitering around the doorway. "We need privacy, gentlemen. I'll keep you appraised."

"Yes, ma'am," they all said at once and scattered away.

Michael returned to Cate's room with everything Anne had

requested, including a bathing tub he filled with warm water from buckets Cal and Cookie provided. Upon Anne's orders, he set up a privacy screen and a chair. Unwilling to leave his daughter, he sat on the other side of the screen while Anne helped Cate remove her clothes and step into the bath.

"Ouch! It burns here...and there," Cate cried out softly.

Michael cringed.

Water splashed, and Anne murmured comforting words. After an interminable time, Anne pushed aside the screen and helped Cate, who was swathed in a coverlet, onto the bed. She opened a tin of ointment and started rubbing it into scratches.

Michael turned away, moved to the window, and gripped the sash.

When she was done, Anne lifted a nightgown over Cate's head and down her body. She fashioned a sling and helped Cate slip her arm into it, then propped her up on her pillows and pulled the covers up around her waist. Michael walked to the side of the bed and studied his daughter. The color had returned to her face that had been spared any disfiguring wounds.

She smiled at him, and he winked.

Cookie knocked on the door frame. "I brought a cup of chamomile tea. Thought it might help."

Anne took the cup from him. "What a dear man you are."

Cookie's tanned cheeks flushed as he left. Michael had never seen the man turn red, and he stifled a laugh.

Cate finished her tea, set the cup on the bedside table, and stretched her good arm over her head. Her expression became serious. "Papa, I cannot tell you how sorry I am."

Michael held up his hand. "We'll save that discussion for another time. Right now, I only want to look at you."

"But that would be awkward." She grinned. "Papa, would you do something for me? Cookie left before I could ask."

How could he deny those beguiling green eyes? He nodded.

"I would love a piece of the apple pie Cookie made last evening."

Anne giggled.

"I'll be back straightaway." Michael hurried from the room, across the house, and out the back door to the kitchen.

Cookie stopped stirring a pot on the stove. "Yes?"

"Cate wants a piece of your apple pie."

The man beamed as if he had been presented a handful of Spanish dollars. "She might care for some milk with it."

Michael waited for Cookie to put the pie and milk on a tray. When he reached Cate's bedroom, he stopped in his tracks and placed the tray on a table by the door.

His daughter, now sound asleep, lay on her side. Anne, also asleep, cuddled next to her with her knees cupped under Cate's knees. Anne had removed her shoes and stockings, and her dainty pink toes peeked out from under her hem.

His heart swelled with so much love, it might burst. Anne was his, and he meant to make that plain to her. He would do whatever it took for her to marry him.

Sitting on the corner of the bed, he removed his boots. Trying not to disturb his ladies, he sidled his body across the bed and cupped Anne's body with his own, curling his knees into hers. He stretched his arm out and rested it across them both.

Anne stirred and murmured, "Our wee lass is asleep."

"Sleep, my love. I'm here."

Thank You, Lord, for this blessing. If it is within Your will, I pray that we become a family soon.

He had a lot to think about and much to do before that could come about.

CHAPTER 25

$\mathcal{M}$ichael waited three endless days before heading for town. During that time, he shared with Cate his offer of marriage to Anne. The news overjoyed Cate, who was healing quickly after her ordeal. Without too many details, he explained Anne's devastating reaction to his offer but made it clear he would make it his life's mission to change her mind. Cate wholeheartedly approved.

He had taken great pains with his toilet, wearing a new dark-blue waistcoat with gold buttons. As he was leaving the house, Cate made sure his crisp cravat was tied properly. She kissed him on both cheeks and blessed his mission.

Thunder rumbled in the distance, and the heaviness and smell of showers hung in the air. He had not thought to bring his sealskin coat. His ironed breeches and new stockings would not fare well in the rain.

On the trail, he practiced what he would say to Anne and how. His approach was crucial. He was not far from town when his horse snorted and shook her head. He sniffed. The distinctive odor of burning pine permeated the air. A forest fire? He prodded his horse forward and looked across the valley. A blue-gray cloud of smoke lingered off to the west, in the direction of the Cherokee village.

Urging his horse into a gallop, he made for the village. The closer he got, the stronger the smell and the heavier the smoke. The villagers had gathered what they could carry and hurried to the other side of the river that bordered their land.

Michael waved to John and Henry. Both on horseback, they helped the stragglers ford the waist-deep waters. He came upon a white-haired woman shuffling out of one of the cabins. Bent over from brittle bones, she clasped a toddler with one hand and a basket with the other. The little boy wore only a breech-cloth and a shell necklace that reached down to his chubby belly. His limpid brown eyes held no fright but stoicism far beyond his tender age.

Michael dismounted. "Come with me, grandmother. I'll see you to safety."

"Thank you, Michael." Her smile softened the myriad lines crisscrossing her sagging skin and exposed missing front teeth.

He bundled the fragile woman into his arms and gently placed her onto his horse. He picked up the little boy and settled him in front of her. The basket could not have been heavier if it had been filled with rocks. How could someone that fragile carry so much?

At the river, he waded into the water, guiding his horse and precious cargo to the other side where the woman's family gathered her and the child into their arms.

John and Henry made their way through the crowd to Michael.

"Do you know where the fire started?" Michael asked as he mounted his horse.

John patted his horse's neck. "There was lightning two nights ago. Sometimes it hits and smolders until it flames."

A gust of wind shot across the river, bending the saplings at the edge of the water.

"The wind will make things worse. I must find out where the fire is and how much it encompasses." Michael nudged his horse. "I'll head northwest."

Henry's horse bobbed her head, and he tightened his grip on the reins. "John and I will go with you."

"Good. Before we go, would you send someone to my house...tell my brother to be at the ready to keep Cate and the others safe?"

After Henry did Michael's bidding, the three of them sought the fire. They had traveled a couple of miles when the smoke became so dense, Michael pulled off his cravat and wound it around his head, covering his mouth and nose. Finally, they ventured upon flames that had engulfed the forest as far as they could see. The snapping of sap-filled pine branches, the roaring of flames licking up the trunks of giant oaks, and the crashing of charred trees falling to the ground were deafening. Michael spotted a doe and her fawn racing near the edge of the fire. Wild-eye and disoriented, they sped in several directions before hurtling out of the burning under-brush to safety.

Soon, the blast of heat, the smoke, and the ashes falling like heavy snow forced Michael and the others to flee. A gust of wind barreled around them, blowing the flames in the opposite direction.

A safe distance from the fire, Michael pulled down his mask. "This wind keeps whipping the fire around. I can't get a handle on how big it is or where it's headed."

"It's moving west again," John yelled through the crackling and popping noises.

Toward the sawmill.

~

*A*nne stood at her shop window searching the street for Katherine and Christopher. They were late, which was unlike them. She shrugged and sat down at the work table where she finished sewing on buttons for a waistcoat.

With a jolt of vivid memory, she recalled the moment three days ago when she awoke after a nap with Cate to find Michael lying next to her. She trembled as she remembered how heavy and warm his arm had been draped over her. She had enjoyed the sensations so much, she had pretended to be asleep just to have more time with him.

The pain from their earlier parting after she had rejected Michael's proposal had soaked into every fiber of her being. A miserable wreck, she had hardly slept or eaten since. Did she truly love her dream more than she loved Michael? Had she chosen her craft over a loving man and his daughter? Was there no way to attain both? In her fervent prayers, she had entreated the Lord for answers to those questions.

The shop door opened, and Sheriff Grant entered, his expression serious. "Good morning, Miss Forbes."

She put her work on the table. "Good morning, sheriff. How may I help you?"

He paused in the doorway, his hand on the knob. "I've come to warn you that there is a forest fire near Grace Holler."

Her stomach muscles tightened. That was why the twins had not come to work.

"The fire's a large one. Not headed this way, though the wretched wind keeps pushing it in all directions."

What of Michael, Cate, and Cal? Their home? The sawmill?

"What should I do?"

"Keep on working. I'll send someone by to let you know if it starts moving in this direction." He glanced over his shoulder. "If it comes to it, we must evacuate the town. There's a grotto, a cave of sorts, down by the river that would provide a shelter.

Follow the others there—if it comes to it, as I said." He tapped his hat.

"Thank you for the warning. Is there a way to know how the occupants of Grace Holler have fared?"

"'fraid not. Not until the fire is out. One thing is in our favor, though." He stared at the darkening sky. "It feels as if we'll have rain sometime today. We can only pray."

When he closed the door, Anne sat back down in a chair, but try as she might, she could not bring herself to sew. In between pacing the front room, she rearranged bolts of material and wrapped several pieces of finished work in brown paper and string.

She walked outside and into the street. In the distance, an ominous cloud had formed, silhouetting the chapel steeple. Thunder rumbled, and a gust of wind whipped around her petticoats. At the front of the mercantile, the owner conversed with a handful of men who pointed to the cloud. Anne had no experience of forest fires, but the sky seemed to darken by the minute. Chills ran up and down her spine as she scurried back inside. She made a cup of tea and had sat down in the back room to drink it when one of the entrance doors flew open.

"Anne! Anne!" Iris called out.

In the doorway, the older woman leaned heavily on her maid. Amelia huddled beside them, her eyes wide.

Anne rose so quickly she almost knocked over her tea cup. "Won't you come in?"

Iris shook her head, her complexion a sickly gray. "No. We must go. The fire is headed toward town."

"Please, Miss Forbes, we must hurry." Helen put her arm around Iris and headed out to the street.

"Yes, please hurry. It's unnerving out here." Amelia waved Anne toward them.

The women's collective panic drove all thoughts from

Anne's mind, and she ran outside and slammed the shop doors. "Where are we going?"

Helen looked back over her shoulder. "To Welch Cave, just out of town and by the river. It's not far."

Fighting panic, Anne followed. Though it was midafternoon, the sky had grown as dark as at dusk. The air reeked of charred wood. The wind ripped flowers from their pots, pushed debris over the crushed granite, and rocked the chairs lined in front of the mercantile.

At the end of the street where it joined the road leading to town, Iris pointed to clusters of townspeople scurrying down a hill and following along the river. "The grotto is that way. About a half mile."

At the bottom of the hill, a rush of wind nearly toppled Iris. Amelia and Helen strengthened their hold on her and supported her between them.

"My tools!" Anne shouted and clamped her hand on her mobcap that threatened to fly off. "I must go back and get them."

"No. No. It's not safe," Amelia called out.

Iris held out her arms. "Please, dear, don't go."

"I must. They are my livelihood. It's taken me a lifetime to pay for them." She hastened back up the hill. "It won't take me but a few minutes," she yelled over her shoulder.

She ran back up the hill and quickly reached the middle of the main street, now eerily deserted. Inside her shop, she grabbed the shears from the work table and stuffed them into a satchel along with needles, pins, a second pair of shears, hanks of linen thread and their ivory winders, and thimbles.

Was retrieving her tools reckless? Would losing them prove unbearable, or was this another one of the poor decisions she had made lately?

She ran outside, and the moment she reached the opposite side of the street, a huge black billow of smoke and ashes spiraled through the air as if belched from a blacksmith's forge. She fell to her knees, coughing and sputtering. She grabbed her mobcap and pressed it against her nose and mouth. Her eyes watered, and tears rolled down her cheeks. She could not see her hand in front of her face.

Where was she? Which way should she move?

Michael would know. If he were here, he'd take care of her. Was he safe?

Lord, please, guard over him, Cate, and Cal.

She staggered back onto her feet and chose a direction, cautiously placing one foot in front of the other. Clutching the satchel in one hand, she waved the other arm back and forth in front of her. She had taken only a few steps when she tripped, slammed her head against something, and sprawled out onto the ground.

She maintained her grip on the satchel until the world went black.

CHAPTER 26

$\mathcal{A}$t the mill, Michael found Cal working alongside the men as they doused logs and newly cut planks with water.

"Cate's in the office with Cookie," Cal called out as he passed a bucket along the chain of men.

When he entered the office, Cate grabbed him around his waist. "Papa. You're here."

Cookie rose from the desk. "Right glad we are of it too."

"I'm all right, Kitten. But if you keep squeezing me like that, I won't be able to breathe."

She pulled away and gave him a tremulous smile. "Uncle Cal said we are to go to the lake if the fire comes here."

Michael cupped her cheek with his hand. "That's the plan. But we've put some things into place to keep the fire away."

She raised a brow.

"Mainly, we've created a break...a kind of barrier...a flattened, clear patch of ground twenty feet wide around the perimeter of the mill."

"Our house?" she asked.

"The land has been cleared around it too."

Burning ashes floating through the air posed a problem, but he chose not to mention anything about that to Cate.

Bramble jumped up from lying in a corner and growled, and the hackles across his back stiffened.

Horse hooves pounded outside, and a voice called out, "'Lo the office."

Michael stepped out the door. "What is it, Franklin?"

The man, one of Michael's employees, took a moment to catch his breath. "I'm to tell you that the fire shifted again."

"Where to?"

"Toward town."

Anne!

Michael ran down the steps. "Franklin, let me have your horse."

He waited for the man to dismount, then jumped up and threw his leg over the mare. He wrapped the reins around his hands and turned the animal around. "Cal, take care of things here. Make sure Cate is safe."

Cal put his hand on Cate's shoulder. "I will, Michael, but don't you want to take some of the men with you?"

"No need to put them in harm's way. It will be easier for me to get in and out quickly if I'm alone. Besides, everyone should be sheltered in Welch Cave by now."

At least, that was his hope.

Cate handed him her kerchief. "Here, Papa. And take Bramble. I'll feel better if he's with you."

"All right, Kitten." He tucked the kerchief into his waistcoat and signaled to the dog. "With me."

He spurred his horse, and he and Bramble left the mill at gallop speed. The fire was encroaching fast toward the turnoff road to the town. To the north, flames engulfed rows of grapevines, the fields of wildflowers, and the surrounding cedar trees.

Would lives be lost in this fire? What would his beloved

mountains look like when this was all over? The questions sickened him.

A black cloud whirled overhead, turning day into night and heating the air, making it difficult to breathe. He would have to skirt around the edge of town and enter from the opposite direction. That meant scaling a treacherous ravine with boulders and patches of falling rocks.

He made a mask of Cate's kerchief. "Come, Bramble."

Picking their way through the rugged terrain, Michael clasped the reins tighter. Twice, rocks loosened under his horse's hooves, and she shied. The way became so craggy, he had to dismount and lead the way. The moment they finally climbed up a hill and onto the town road, a misty rain began to fall.

"Thank you, Lord," he whispered.

With his eyes burning from the smoke, he crossed the road and made his way down to the grotto. By the time he reached it, the soft rain had shifted into a steady fall. He dismounted, entered the huge cave, and scanned the crowd of about fifty. Right away, he spotted Iris and Amelia. Where was Anne? His heart pounding in his throat, he searched the faces again.

"Michael. Oh, Michael," Amelia called out. She shook from head to toe.

"Where's Anne?" he said, holding her by her shoulders.

She wrung her hands. "She...she isn't with us. We were on our way here, but she went back."

Iris joined them. "To her shop."

Struggling not to panic, Michael could barely grasp what they were saying. "Why on earth?"

"To get her tools," Iris answered. "We haven't seen her since. The sheriff wouldn't let anyone go. It's too dangerous."

"Well, I'm going. Look after my horse, will you? We had a rough time getting here, and she's spent." He took off running.

"To get here, we took the cut in between the two buildings across from her shop," Iris yelled behind him.

What was Anne thinking? Once he found her, would he shake her or kiss her?

Anger and frustration roiled inside him. And fear—an insidious emotion that threatened his judgement. He looked down at Bramble, and a thought struck him. He reached inside his waistcoat and withdrew Anne's handkerchief that he carried next to his heart.

Pressing it to Bramble's nose, he shouted, "Find. Find Anne."

The dog breathed in the scent and shot off up the hill, sniffing the trail Anne and the others had taken. He bounded across the road and stopped at the entrance to Anne's shop. He hesitated, sniffing the ground one way and then the other.

"What is it, boy?"

Bramble stretched up his neck and howled a loud and haunting sound.

Michael's heart plummeted. Did the dog sense something terrible?

Bramble stiffened and launched his body toward the potter's shop two doors down. Michael scrambled after him. When he rounded the corner of the building, there lay Anne, her body still and the side of her face wet with blood.

CHAPTER 27

*M*ichael fell to his knees and gently pulled Anne into his arms. "My darling, my precious Anne."

Her body was cold and so still, he feared the worst. His heart cracked inside his chest.

Anne's eyes fluttered open, and she moaned. "Michael?"

"I'm here, my love. You are safe now." Tears streamed down his face, and he whispered, "Thank You, God. Thank You."

Anne raised her hand to her head. "It hurts."

He moved her hand away and held it to his lips. "You may have hit it when you fell."

Suddenly, a heavy rain poured down, clearing the smoke from the air.

"Let's get you out of this."

He gathered Anne into his arms, but she reached out her arm. "My tools."

Exasperated, he knelt, and she pulled the satchel across her chest. He carried her into her shop and up the stairs, where he placed her on her mattress. Bramble followed them and settled on the bed at Anne's feet.

"Good boy. Stay and watch after her while I fetch water and bandages."

He raced down the steps and threw open cupboard doors until he found her medicine kit. He grabbed a pail and ran outside to fill it from the pump. Juggling the water pail and the small chest, he bounded up the stairs.

"I'm back, sweetling. I'll care for you."

She blinked, and her bottom lip trembled. "You called me sweetling. Aren't you angry with me?"

"I-I..." He gulped. "Never, ever again."

She closed her eyes. "I'm happy. It hurt terribly knowing you were out of sorts with me."

His words had hurt her. Would that he could take them back.

Using a cloth from the medicine chest, he cleaned the wound on her forehead. "No stitches needed, but you will have a nasty bruise."

As he started spreading the ointment, Anne whimpered.

"I know it pains you, my love."

"It was so dark, Michael, I couldn't see where I was going. I'm not certain what I ran into. It was all very frightening." Her eyes wide, she gripped the front of his shirt.

He loosened her grasp on the material. "It's over, my darling. Don't think on it. Let me finish binding the wound and get you out of these wet clothes."

It took everything he had not to lean down and kiss the abrasion, so he caressed the other side of her forehead. After he wrapped a bandage around her head, he tugged a quilt out from under Bramble and covered her with it, pulling it up to her neck. Trying to preserve her modesty, he started removing her rain-drenched, soiled clothes that he threw onto the floor. Next, he searched her armoire and found a nightgown with ribbons at the neck and sleeves. He slipped the gown over her head and down her body.

After he fastened the ribbons, he met her gaze. She had not blushed, but questions filled her eyes. Despite his effort to maintain her privacy, the brief glimpse of her he had gotten compelled an honest answer.

"You are wonderfully made, my love, from head to toe." The passion of his body matched the passion of his words.

He pulled the wet cover from the bed and replaced the bloody pillow with a fresh one. He pulled a clean cover over her once more and settled in a chair beside the bed.

"I know you are tired, but you suffered a head wound and mustn't sleep for a while. I'll make you a cup of tea soon." He picked up a book from her side table. "*Gulliver's Travels*. One of my favorites. Shall I read to you, or shall we talk?"

Anne reached her arm from under the covers and held out her hand. "I should like to talk."

Was he prepared for the conversation ahead?

He covered her hand with his. "All right."

"When last we parted, it was after Cate had fallen from the tree. It was such trauma for us both, we avoided speaking about our...troubles." She twined her fingers through his. "But I do remember distinctly that, once she was safe, you lay with us on Cate's bed. What were you thinking then?"

He circled her palm with his thumb. "I prayed that God would hear my prayer and bring us together as a family."

"I have prayed as well." She sighed. "I would like nothing better than for us to be a family."

"You want to marry me?" Michael's heart leapt. "What about your work? After all, you risked your life to save your tools."

The thought tortured him. If work meant that much to her, was he selfish enough to make her give it up? Wasn't he supposed to be the provider with his wife devoting herself to the family? He knew from his first wife what running a household would take. Could Anne manage family and work?

Of course she could. She was a wonderfully accomplished woman.

He moved onto the bed, lay beside her, and slipped his arms around her waist. Bramble hopped onto the floor and curled up on the rug beside Anne's rocking chair. Michael stared at the chair. So much had occurred and their lives had changed since he had purchased it for her. It seemed ages ago.

"If you agree to be my wife, I will do anything...anything...to make you happy. We can compromise. Maybe we could build you a shop at home. If that doesn't suit, maybe I could move in here with you." He hesitated. "No, that wouldn't work. Where would we put Cate and Bramble? Though he seems comfortable where his is. What about the mill? I could ask Cal to take it over. We'd have to get a new bed. This one is way too small for me."

Anne giggled.

"I'm babbling, aren't I?"

"You are and I adore you for it." She caressed his beard and ran her fingers down his jaw. "You need to ken this, I love you more than my life. More than my work. In my heart, I feel that God put us together on the trail from Philadelphia. We traversed valleys and struggled through trials, but He brought us through all of that so that I might call you my husband. My dear, braw man."

Michael shook from the emotions shooting through his body. Anne's every word echoed his hopes and dreams.

"What is *braw*?" he asked, bringing her fingers to his lips and kissing each one individually.

"It means excellent, fine looking." She brushed back a tendril of hair from his face.

He beamed. "I like that. What is the Scottish word for beautiful?"

"*Aoife*, pronounced *ee-fa*. Or an easier word is *bonnie*."

Unable to wait a moment longer, he captured her lips with

his. The feel of her, the smell of her, the way her lips opened to his, set the world spinning. "My bonnie lass."

They kissed and cuddled, touched and hugged until Michael felt compelled to restrain their intimacy. He slid from the bed, and unable to resist, he leaned down for another kiss. Gazing into her soft-brown eyes, it took all of his strength to tuck the covers around her and head for the door. Bramble refused his gesture to follow him, jumped back on the bed, and snuggled at Anne's feet.

Pausing in the doorway, Michael gazed at Anne once more. "Rest for now, my sweetling. We'll talk tomorrow."

He closed the door behind him and lifted a silent prayer. *Thank You, Lord, for Your many blessings. You fulfilled our prayers and transformed our long and treacherous road into a trail to love.*

EPILOGUE

Standing on their front porch holding hands with Cate, Anne shaded her eyes with her hand and searched the road leading up to the house. She let go of Cate's hand and massaged the muscles that had knotted in her back off and on for days.

Michael stood beside her, cuddling their two-year-old son, Jacob Daniel Jonathan, on his hip. They had named their beautiful, ebony-haired boy Jacob after Michael's father, Daniel after hers, and Jonathan, a name Cate insisted on because she favored it. Anne leaned into her husband, reveling in his warmth and strength.

He massaged the small of her back. "It pains you, sweetling?"

"A wee bit," she admitted.

Cal and a very pregnant Amelia sat nearby in ladder-back chairs, their eyes only for each other. After a proper mourning period and an intense courtship, the two had married and had not waited any time to become parents.

Anne looked over her shoulder at Iris. She had fallen asleep in the willow branch rocker. Bramble lay beside her, and they both snored softly.

Almost everyone she loved gathered around her. The rest of them would arrive soon, according to one of Michael's employees, who had ridden from town to let them know William, Gail, and David were on their way.

"How much longer, Michael?" Anne asked.

Michael handed Jacob to Cate, wrapped an arm around Anne's waist, and rested a hand on her distended stomach. "I know how excited you are, my darling, but don't get overwrought."

She gazed up at him, and as always, her legs wobbled at the depth of love for her that shone in his eyes. This handsome, charming, kind, wonderful, and godly man was well and truly hers. God had showered them with His blessings.

"I think I see them," Cate called out.

Anne pushed her spectacles further onto her nose and squinted. "Yes! I see them."

Michael tipped up her chin and looked into her eyes again. "You're trembling, Anne. And I can feel that you are tempted to take off running, but you mustn't."

The baby stretched, making its presence known, and Michael curved a protective hand underneath Anne's belly. Would they have another son with Michael's hazel eyes and black hair, or would it be a girl with Anne's brown eyes and hair?

She rose on her tiptoes, cupped his beard with her hand, and kissed his lips. "Yes, dear, as you say."

Nearly dancing from one foot to the next, she watched as William's wagon neared. "I'm thrilled beyond measure that Gail recovered and decided to join us here. How much has David changed, and will he even remember me? I cannot wait to tell William that my shop will be his."

For four years, she had lived her dream, first in the shop in town, and then in a small building Michael had constructed next to their home after Jacob was born. The twins, Katherine and Christopher, had kept the town business going and had recently left Graniteville to set up their own business in a new settlement thirty miles away. With the baby on the way, it made sense for her to accept only very special sewing projects in the future.

Suddenly, a pain ripped its way across Anne's back. She groaned and her knees buckled. Michael picked her up, carried her inside, and lay her on their bed.

Suzanne Marie Harrigan came into the world six hours later. Cuddling her newborn daughter, Anne twirled her finger around a tuft of the baby's auburn-tinted hair and smiled at the dear people who had circled her bed after giving Michael and her time alone with their precious girl.

"You arranged quite a reception for us, dear sister." William chuckled.

Anne reached out and held his hand. "You are truly here." Tears filled her eyes.

"It's our own dancing ground," she said to Michael, who hovered next to her on the side of the bed. "Everyone has come home along their different trails. God is good."

Did you enjoy this book? We hope so!
Would you take a quick minute to leave a review where you purchased the book?
It doesn't have to be long. Just a sentence or two telling what you liked about the story!

Receive a FREE ebook and get updates when new Wild Heart books release: https://wildheartbooks.org/newsletter

ABOUT THE AUTHOR

Susan F. Craft retired after a 45-year career in writing, editing, and communicating in business settings.

She authored the historical romantic suspense trilogy *Women of the American Revolution—The Chamomile, Laurel,* and *Cassia. The Chamomile* and *Cassia* received national Illumination Silver Awards. *The Chamomile* was named by the Southern Independent Booksellers Alliance as an Okra Pick and was nominated for a Christy Award.

She collaborated with the International Long Riders' Guild Academic Foundation to compile *An Equestrian Writer's Guide* (www.lrgaf.org), including almost everything you'd ever want to know about horses.

An admitted history nerd, she enjoys painting, singing,

listening to music, and sitting on her porch watching geese eat her daylilies. She most recently took up the ukulele.

AUTHOR'S NOTES

I've often admitted that I enjoy researching more than writing. I've spent hundreds of hours in libraries, at Revolutionary War reenactments and museums, and wandering around sites that I've featured in my novels. I cannot count the hours I've spent on the internet lost in rabbit warrens of information where one tidbit would send me off from one direction to the next.

These are some historical tidbits I've woven into *Trail to Love*:

Basswood

Because of its soft, uniform texture, this wood lends itself to sculpting, especially musical instruments. Its sap contains sugar that Native Americans boiled and made into a drink. They used the cambium layers to make soups and bread, the bark for bandages, and the fiber for ropes, baskets, belts, fishnets, and house mats.

Beloved Woman

Beloved Woman or *ghi gua* is the title that the Cherokee gave to recognize and honor a woman who showed great heroism on the battlefield as a *War Woman*, and who later advised war councils and provided wisdom to her village.

Colonial American Currency

The English pound was the primary form of currency in the American colonies. The Spanish dollar, an unofficial currency in the seventeenth and eighteenth centuries, had a distinctive design and consistent silver content. In order to make change, the soft silver coin was cut (using a hammer and chisel) into eight pie-shaped pieces or *bits*. The phrase *two bits, four bits, six bits, a dollar* came about from the Spanish dollar. Pirates called them *pieces of eight*.

Colonists also used the barter system, exchanging goods and services for such things as tobacco leaves, land, deer and beaver skins, and shells.

Dancing Grounds

These were the places where multiple paths and lanes came together in the Blue Ridge Mountains. People would regularly gather on these grounds to dance by moonlight. The dancing grounds still exist today.

Female Archers (Archeresses) in Scotland

Michael is astonished by Anne's prowess as an archeress. Archery has long been a popular sport for women in Scotland and was one of the first to allow women to participate. Its roots come from the history of Scottish female warriors/archers that goes back centuries. For example, the Countess of Ross led her troops during battles with the English in 1297. Isobel, Countess of Buchan, fought for Robert the Bruce, was imprisoned for four years, and afterwards retired to a convent. Women fought among the regular soldiers of the Scots army that marched on Newcastle in 1644 during the English Civil War.

The Gaelic word for warrior woman is *banlaoch*.

Kanuchi

This is a favorite sweet among the Cherokee. It is made from powdered hickory nuts and boiled rice rolled into balls.

Lumberjack

The word *lumberjack* did not come into use until 1830 in Canada. Prior to that, they were called lumbermen, loggers, timber beasts, and wood hicks. Most of them traditionally wore shirts of red and black checks. Men who drove logs down a river were known as river rats, river hogs, river pigs, or catty-men.

Philadelphia Streets

In 1751, Benjamin Franklin, among many other names, was known as the founding father of public trash collection. He proposed the idea of daily cleaning Philadelphia streets of the accumulation of mud, animal carcasses, rotting vegetables, manure, and chamber pot waste. (Gross!) I made up the idea of using water from pumps to clean the streets twice a day.

Tree House

When researching the kinds of trees Michael would work with at his sawmill, I discovered a picture of a family living inside a tree in the Appalachian Mountains during the Depression era. Fascinated, I tumbled down a rabbit trail that led me to a myriad of information about and pictures of families in the United States, especially the Pacific Northwest, living in the trunks of giant redwoods. I had to include this in my novel.

Watch-night

This was a Methodist practice of gathering to devote themselves to prayer, reflection, and encouragement to the holy life. Charles Wesley attended a meeting on April 24, 1741, and was inspired to write two watch-night hymns. Eventually, he wrote nineteen hymns, eleven of which were printed in a pamphlet in 1790 entitled *Hymns for the Watch-night*. Over time, the meetings changed from monthly to quarterly and eventually became a New Year's Eve tradition.

ACKNOWLEDGMENTS

I offer my sincere appreciation to the Oconaluftee Indian Village in Cherokee, North Carolina. They have recreated a 1760s village with traditional dwellings, work areas, and sacred ritual places. During the numerous times I visited the village, the sights, sounds, and smells enthralled me. I witnessed the people making a canoe, sculpting pottery, hand-fashioning beadwork, weaving cane baskets, and forming thistle into darts for a blowgun. As a history nerd, I could not have been happier.

I also thank the Cherokee Nation for the fabulous videos, *Cherokee Word of the Week*, where Cherokee words are spoken, spelled out, and defined. The site helped me create names for my Cherokee characters.

My heartfelt gratitude goes to Rudy Mancke (Rudolph Ernest Mancke III). He was curator of natural history at the South Carolina State Museum, host naturalist of the South Carolina Educational Television program *NatureScene* for twenty-five years, and naturalist in residence at the University of South Carolina. His love and enthusiasm for nature were infectious. A walking encyclopedia and treasure trove of knowledge, for years he generously answered my many questions as I researched for my novels. Sadly, Rudy passed last year (2023).

And, of course, I extend heartfelt gratitude to my Lord from who all blessings flow.

Soli Deo Gloria.

If you love historical romance, check out the other Wild Heart books!

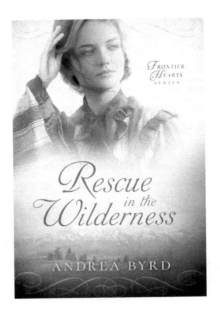

Rescue in the Wilderness by Andrea Byrd

William Cole cannot forget the cruel burden he carries, not with the pock marks that serve as an outward reminder. Riddled with guilt, he assumed the solitary life of a long hunter, traveling into the wilds of Kentucky each year. But his quiet existence is changed in an instant when, sitting in a tavern, he overhears a man offering his daughter—and her virtue—to the winner of the next round of cards. William's integrity and desire for redemption will not allow him to sit idly by while such an injustice occurs.

Lucinda Gillespie has suffered from an inexplicable illness her entire life. Her father, embarrassed by her condition, has subjected her to a lonely existence of abuse and confinement. But faced with the ultimate betrayal on the eve of her eighteenth birthday, Lucinda quickly realizes her trust is better placed in the hands of the mysterious man who appears at her door. Especially when he offers her the one thing she never thought would be within her grasp—freedom.

In the blink of an eye, both lives change as they begin the difficult, danger-fraught journey westward on the Wilderness Trail. But can they overcome their own perceptions of themselves to find love and the life God created them for?

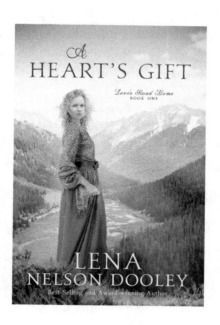

A Heart's Gift by Lena Nelson Dooley

Is a marriage of convenience the answer?

Franklin Vine has worked hard to build the ranch he inherited into one of the most successful in the majestic Colorado mountains. If only he had an heir to one day inherit the legacy he's building. But he was burned once in the worst way, and he doesn't plan to open his heart to another woman. Even if that means he'll eventually have to divide up his spread among the most loyal of his hired hands.

When Lorinda Sullivan is finally out from under the control of men who made all the decisions in her life, she promises herself she'll never allow a man to make choices for her again. But without a home in the midst of a hard Rocky Mountain winter, she has to do something to provide for her infant son.

A marriage of convenience seems like the perfect arrangement, yet the stakes quickly become much higher than either of them ever planned. When hearts become entangled, the increasing danger may change their lives forever.

~

Lone Star Ranger by Renae Brumbaugh Green

Elizabeth Covington will get her man.

And she has just a week to prove her brother isn't the murderer Texas Ranger Rett Smith accuses him of being. She'll show the good-looking lawman he's wrong, even if it means setting out on a risky race across Texas to catch the real killer.

Rett doesn't want to convict an innocent man. But he can't let the Boston beauty sway his senses to set a guilty man free. When Elizabeth follows him on a dangerous trek, the Ranger vows to keep her safe. But who will protect him from the woman whose conviction and courage leave him doubting everything—even his heart?